THE TIME KEEPER

Kevin E. Cropp

Mauri, Nancy, Alex, Sara,

I hope y...

book as much as Hedly

I liked your slide show

from 6th Serengeti.

Best Wishes,

Kevin E. Cropp

A COPPER PRESS BOOK

Published by Copper Press
Copper Press
8207 Rhiannon Rd., Raleigh, NC, 27613, U.S.A.
Copper Press registered offices: Raleigh, NC.

The Time Keeper / Kevin E. Cropp
ISBN 0-9760506-1-7
Library of Congress Control Number: 2005921866

Printed and bound in the United States of America

This book is dedicated to my mother.

Chapter 1

WHEN LINDA WAILS found herself living on a dead-end street, next door to a black cat and mourning doves in the bushes, she knew her life had gone awry. The realtor failed to mention the cat or the birds and for good reason. What difference did it make? Who else besides Linda Wails would care what color a cat is and what type of bird lives in the bushes?

On inspection of the neighbor's pet she found a pink tongue, beady yellow eyes, and an otherwise colorless cat. If he crossed her path on the dead-end street, which was often, she turned the car around and headed back home, regardless of where she was going or how important it was to get there. Nothing was so important to warrant crossing the path of a black cat.

The mourning dove lived in the bushes outside her window. She thought it was bad luck to hear the call of a dove before the sun came up, and she heard it every day. I could never figure out how a small gray bird could cause anyone so much distress. It was just another bad omen in the mind of Linda Wails; around every corner she saw bad luck lurking.

She went to great lengths not to test fate. On her order the moving company wrapped the mirrors twice; we always left a building by the same door we entered; if salt was spilled she threw a pinch over her shoulder; a penny tails up stayed where it lie. I listened to her fanatic notions, but never believed any of them. I thought it was ludicrous to let superstition rule your life.

It seemed that our move to the sand hills of North Carolina was a bad decision. There were signs of it everywhere. "I might as well lean a ladder over the front door and squeeze under it every morning," Linda said about her new life. She complained incessantly; blaming the realtor for not telling her about the cat and the birds; she blamed her husband for making her move to a god-forsaken place with so much sand, so few trees, and no water. I listened to her and sometimes I just stared at her, looking for the dark clouds looming over her head. But maybe she was right, maybe there was something to it after all, because bad things did seem to happen to her—all the time.

Our first year in the sand hills a strange incident occurred, just the kind of thing that could be faultlessly blamed on a black cat. After a long day of working in the yard, which her husband Robert groomed as fine as any golf course, his life came to a halt. He mumbled some inaudible words and his face hit the table. Linda was erratic. She screamed at me to call an ambulance as she lifted his head. I thought he was dead, and so did she. The combination of stepping on a bottle cap and spraying weed killer was going to take the life of Robert Wails—bizarre.

The doctors told us that a cut on his foot had allowed the chemicals he was spraying to enter his blood stream and had clouded his brain. There was nothing to do but wait. So we waited. For days we sat in the hospital and waited for him to wake up. While her husband was on a respirator, Linda made a list of all the things she wanted to do with him, but never had. When he wakes up we are going to do them, she told herself.

In Memorial Hospital, with her usual business attitude that things must be planned to run smoothly, she began planning—trips to Egypt, Rome, Paris, and smaller affairs like picnic lunches and catamaran rides at Holden Beach, all the things she and her husband had wanted to do together but never had. Her list grew longer and longer every day he remained in a coma, and before she was finished it sounded like they would be gone traveling for years.

Robert woke up three days later with a crushing headache and no recollection whatsoever of the incident. He wondered why she was crying and why the hell he was in a hospital.

That jolt was not enough for Linda Wails to change her life and things around the house were business as usual, except Robert wore shoes when he sprayed pesticide. We went to Sunset Beach for a week that summer and perhaps Linda dreamed she was eating in a Roman bistro, but it was just a hot dog stand on Main Street.

A few more years went by and save a few stitches here and there and a couple close brushes with catastrophe the Wails got along just fine. But at the beginning of Linda's thirty-first year all the black cats, owls, and mourning doves in North Carolina converged on our street. They all came the same day and they never left.

Chapter 2

LINDA'S LIST was long that day—pick up the dry-cleaning, buy some green chilies and cream cheese for the enchiladas, mail the insurance check, call a plumber about the kitchen sink, and book Doctor Snyder's tickets to Paris for him and his wife. She did not need a pad to remind herself of the day's tasks, but wished she did. Her mind went through the list before her feet hit the floor, same as every morning. Linda hated having such a good memory. If only she could forget, just for a little while, maybe she could enjoy the silence.

She walked into the bathroom to get ready for work. She looked at herself in the mirror and wondered why people always told her she was beautiful. Her hair was filthy brown and she wished it were blonde. Her cheekbones were high and angled and she wished they were round and soft giving her face a pleasant smoothness. Linda thought she was entirely too strong to be a beautiful woman.

She leaned forward looking for wrinkles and noticed

the dark iris in each eye and wished they were blue like her sapphire birthstone.

"I am not beautiful at all," she thought, stepping back from the mirror. She had to slouch just a bit to make her whole body fit. Her shoulders were broad, her collar bone defined, rigid, and strong, and she wished she were a petite woman who could wear size four so shopping wouldn't be so hard. She combed the tangles from her hair. It fell down around her shoulders and she decided to cut it off—all of it. Maybe she would look better with one of the trendy new bob hairstyles. She stepped into the shower thinking maybe today will be better after a haircut.

On the way to work, Linda remembered she had forgotten something and knew she was getting old. Linda never forgot anything. Today was the day for her follow-up visit to the cancer clinic. The lab results would be back and in her eyes her fate decided in black and white. The cancer results evaded her completely this morning, and she could not for the life of herself figure out how.

She passed by the hospital one turn before her employer's office and remembered when her husband's life was on hold for three days. Today of all days Linda chose to remember that incident. Her mind went through the long list of dreams she made in the waiting room and the list was the same today—not a single check mark was on it.

With darkness clouding her thoughts as it often did she pictured herself eating prunes and fiber supplements on a tour of the White House for her first real vacation. However, Linda was a very practical woman and before she parked in front of her office she had it all worked out. When we get the second car paid off, we will go on a big trip, she told herself.

Things were hectic at work and she quickly forgot about her husband's near death experience, her dreams, and everything else. Her boss, Doctor Snyder, was seeing double the patients trying to get them out of the way before his vacation to Paris.

Linda thought about her visit to the cancer clinic and started to worry. The thoughts of breast cancer haunted her every day, ever since the visit when they found the lump. She tried to forget about it, but to no avail. It was not that easy.

At one o'clock she walked into the cancer center at Memorial Hospital for the second time in as many weeks. Sitting in the waiting room she went through the remainder of her list of things to do today. I have a hair appointment at four, she thought, and it eased her anxiety. She loved getting her hair cut and wished it would grow faster so she could get it cut more often. It wasn't the actual haircut she loved, but the women that pampered her, did her nails, complimented her, and made her feel pretty.

The lab results were not good—not good at all. After the word cancer she heard nothing else. Her breathing was shallow and the doctor looked like he was standing at the end of a tunnel. The walls of the room caved in and she thought she would be sick. Why me? She asked herself. Why do bad things always happen to me? That was her take on life and this news only reinforced the idea—bad things only happened to Linda Wails.

"Linda, are you all right?" the doctor asked, and she tried to focus on him. The room was spinning. "It will require surgery," were the last words she heard.

She skipped the afternoon of work and the beauty

parlor and went straight home. She wondered just how much surgery the doctor meant. She sat in the yard and looked at her flowers. They will never look pretty again, she told herself. In her eyes her life was doomed. She had cancer.

When I heard the news I immediately thought this would be just the turn of events needed for her to change her life. I thought she dreamed too much and did too little and maybe this would turn things around. I was right about things changing, but was dead wrong as to how.

A month later she underwent a double mastectomy. It is a day I could hardly forget because Linda Wails never returned from the hospital. They sent another woman home in her place, a woman I never loved. The doctors removed not only the offending cancer but her heart as well. They stole her strength, her beauty, and her motherhood.

I learned, and I learned fast, to stay out of her way. I heard no more dreams about far away places. We did not go to the beach for summer vacation. Linda Wails became a recluse and an outcast—a leper with no colony of her own. Her visits to the mirror left her dazed and confused about her womanhood. In my eyes she gave up. She stopped believing that things would get better just because they always do.

She was thirty-one years old then and I was ten. I lost a friend, but more importantly a mother on that day. I was left with only memories of how things used to be around the Wail's house. She wasn't even superstitious any longer. I wished she would go on about the cats and the owls so I could poke fun at her. I wished we could go to the beach and maybe she would remember how much fun we used to have. I wished we could go back to the farm in Virginia and take a tractor ride, just the two of us, so she could remember how beautiful her life used to be. I wished a lot of things, but they never came true.

Eventually I quit trying just like she did and turned on her like a little dog tired of the big one biting at his tail. As the years went by, seven miserable years, I myself forgot what had happened—how things came to be this way. I could hardly remember a day when they were any different; a day when my mother and I could talk, laugh, and love one another. I guess we were both waiting for the other one to wake up, and for some people that takes an awfully big jolt.

Chapter 3

WHEN I AWOKE the shadows were gone from my room; meaning the sun was high and I was late for school. I jumped out of bed, dressed quickly, and ran out back to feed my dog.

The ground was soggy, muddy in places, and my dog Royal was covered in it. He was sitting very still beneath a maple tree, looking up, hoping one of the red breasted warblers would fall and he would have a snack. He turned sharply when he heard me coming and started off full speed in my direction.

"Easy boy," I said, putting my hand out to keep him from jumping on me. I knelt down, rubbed his ears, and let him lick my face. His tail was wagging and his tongue was hanging down to the ground.

Royal was almost eight years old and had been a present from my mother before her impetuous behavior. On Christmas morning she handed me a small green box. Upon opening it I found a leather collar, a blank silver pendant, and a poem. The poem began, "Your best friend I will be, furry and free." Before I finished reading it, the little red puppy was licking my face.

My mother and I decided to name him Royal, after our street, but in time the name took on a host of new meanings, as he had eyes of royal blue and moved with the grace of nobility. He was a brilliant red Siberian Husky, with penetrating eyes, and a distinguished mask; a beautiful dog by anyone's standards.

Royal gulped down the bowl of food I brought him, headed back to the enticing warbler, and I left for school.

I pulled into the school parking lot with four minutes to spare, and my best friend, Cole O'Conner, pulled in right behind me. I jumped out of my jeep and Cole sprang from his car.

"Did you see him?" I asked urgently, wondering if Cole had spotted Mr. Torant, the school vice principal; the man in charge of discipline and safety at Hillcrest High.

"Not yet, but he's here somewhere," Cole said, throwing his backpack over his shoulder and looking around.

It was rumored that prior to coming to our school, Mr. Torant was denied entry into the police academy; someone said he failed the physical.

Cole spotted him first.

"Over there—you see him? Ducked down behind the red Buick," Cole said.

"Where? I don't see him ..." I replied, scanning the parking lot for Mr. Torant.

With a walkie-talkie clipped to the collar of his jacket and out-of-place running shoes on his feet, he was emerging from his hiding place behind a red Buick Le Sabre.

What would transpire in the next two and a half minutes was routine: Mr. Torant would spot us, we would spot him, and a chase would ensue.

"Cole O'Conner, Corey Wails, I want to speak to you," Mr. Torant yelled.

Like a seasoned professional he started out at a fast walk, angling himself between us and the school.

Cole took off. I gave pursuit, and Mr. Torant tried to head us off at the tennis courts.

Cole was ahead of me when we passed the boxwoods; I took the lead at the water fountain. Mr. Torant was just passing the dogwoods when I threw open the back door of the school. I stopped for a moment and looked down the line; there was Mr. Torant, running like the wind, his blazer trailing behind him, his hair flapping in the breeze, all the while yelling into his walkie-talkie. The buzzer hadn't sounded, so Cole and I had not broken a law just yet, but time was of the essence.

Cole flew by me, as I stood transfixed holding the door and staring at Mr. Torant in disbelief that he was about the same age as my father. I couldn't picture Robert Wails doing such a thing. My father would just stand at the door of my first period class and wait for me to come to him. That was after all the only logical way to go about it.

"Wails, you stand right there," Mr. Torant yelled.

I took off after Cole, who had already turned the hall corner and was out of sight. Seconds later I flew through the door of my first period class, hit the brakes, slid a row, and dropped down into my seat right next to Cole.

"Well, well, if it isn't Tweedle Dee and Tweedle Dum," my first period teacher, Mr. Stewart, said drolly.

Just then Mr. Torant burst into the room. He was out of breath, his hair was in disarray, sweaty, and pushed to one side. Smugly, Mr. Torant collected himself, straightened his coat, and pushed his hair back in place.

"I believe you have a couple of late ..." he began, but was cut short by the school's late buzzer.

The pupils were laughing. Unbeknownst to Mr. Torant his intimidation was like a Spanish terrier. Cole and I watched his face go flat and his smug look disappear. The excitement had been for naught; so caught up in it all, Mr. Torant forgot to listen for the bell.

Mr. Stewart was seated on a stool at the front of the room. He was wearing denim blue jeans and a loose fitting shirt open at the neck. He had a boot propped up on the desk in front of him and was sipping on his coffee like a man who was enjoying his morning.

"What's that you were sayin' John?" Mr. Stewart said slyly, and looked up at me and Cole. I couldn't help but smile.

"Nothing," Mr. Torant snapped, and turned his eyes to me and Cole.

"Corey Wails, don't let me catch you running in the halls," he said.

I felt like snapping to attention and giving a hearty salute to the commanding officer, but thought better of the idea.

He turned to Cole. "Mr. O'Conner, you need to slow down in the parking lot. This isn't a race track son."

"Ey. Ey. Cap'n," Cole said, but refrained from saluting, which probably saved him a trip to the principal's office.

Mr. Torant turned on his heels and slammed the door

on his way out.

School went by slow and boring, as we shuffled from room to room at ten minutes past every hour like cows still on the hoof. But there was one class I looked forward to—the one I shared with my girlfriend, Emily Vallent.

She had been my girlfriend for four years, only I had spent the five before that trying to make her so. If we lasted, and someday were married, we would have a story to tell our kids.

The first words spoken to me by Emily were, 'If you were the last boy on Earth, Corey Wails, I wouldn't be your girlfriend.' She said that to me in the fifth grade, and held her stance head strong until the ninth grade, which was the best year of my life. Cole and I wrecked his go-cart into a tree. Cole only crushed his windpipe, but I punctured my liver with a rib and had to be hospitalized. Our homeroom teacher, Mrs. Williams, sent my assignments via Emily. It was just the twist of fate I needed. I never did thank Mrs. Williams, but I'm sure she knew what she was doing.

At any rate, I left the hospital with a healed liver, along with the girl I had spent five years pursuing to no avail. For years, I told myself if only I had Emily, I would never need another thing. In hindsight, Cole and I should have wrecked the go-cart back in the fifth grade.

At 2:30 I dropped down in my seat next to Emily.

"I heard Mr. Torant chased you down again today," she said smiling.

"You should have seen him come into Mr. Stewart's room. His hair was all messed up and he was panting," I replied.

We laughed about it for a minute and then I asked Emily about her trip to visit colleges.

"So how was your week away, I sure missed you," I said smoothly. Emily lit up the room with her smile and her big, blue eyes.

"It was fine, but I wish I knew where you were going to college. It would make it easier for me to decide," Emily said and waited for a reply. When no reply came she continued: "So how was being at home all week while I was gone?" Emily knew that because she had been gone, I had been forced to go home; I usually spent most of my time at her house.

"Terrible. What else is new? It's getting worse Em. You should have seen her yelling at me last night. I honestly think she's gone mad."

"I'm sorry," Emily said, full of remorse for something she wasn't accountable for.

"It's not your fault she's crazy. I just can't wait to get the hell out of here. Mark my words—I'm never coming back."

Emily took my words to heart and looked at me in a peculiar way, wondering if I could leave her so easily too; an inconsequential loss in the battle for freedom.

"Never coming back? Where are you going, Corey?"

"Anywhere. I don't even care at this point."

"Corey. It's not that bad."

"Yeah, not for you," I answered, goaded by the nerve she had to comment on something she knew nothing about, couldn't relate to, and would never understand. "You wanna trade families?"

"No Corey. I don't want to trade families, but what

about me?" Emily said, full of self-interest.

"What about you? Why does this have anything to do with you?" I asked.

Emily made no reply; her answer was in her eyes, and I realized I had missed the point entirely. It had everything to do with her.

The buzzer sounded, signifying the end of the day, and not a minute too soon. I put the conversation out of my mind and focused on the big game tonight.

Chapter 4

RAY CAVANAUGH stood in the doorway of the locker room. At 62 years old he still had the spry look of a ball player. He was tossing a baseball in his left hand; his right was tucked into the belt of his pants. He was moving a wad of tobacco around in his cheek, and thinking—all the games, all the wins, all the losses, and all the memories. There had been hundreds of nights like this one, nights when we met our rivals on the baseball diamond, but none had ever carried equal consequences. Never had we donned our uniforms for what could be our last game. Tonight was the division championship between us and Anson County. We had been in the same spot the year before and it was our team who came up short. We were determined to turn things around this year.

"Manny, you're leading off in center. Fitz, you're hitting second at short. Miller, third, at second base. Posie you're batting clean-up, behind the plate …" Coach Cavanaugh went through the line-up.

But he stopped after eight players. The pitcher, in the number nine spot, would remain a mystery until game time.

"Who's throwing tonight, Coach?" Todd Manny asked with a wide grin.

Cavanaugh made no reply. He only raised his eye brows slightly and kept on tossing the game ball, up and down, up and down. He never revealed who was pitching until he handed them the game ball.

Ray Cavanaugh whipped us into shape our senior year, even more so than the years prior, which was quite an accomplishment.

"What you lack in talent, you'll make up with fitness," he said as we ran sprint after sprint during winter training.

"What you lack in finesse, you'll make up with determination," he yelled as we ran the bases until we hardly felt our cleats touch the bags.

We listened to our coach wholeheartedly, if for no other reason, because on his finger was a ring given only to the winning team of the World Series. Ray Cavanaugh pitched for the 1969 Miracle Mets; a team that fooled the world and won the pennant with all odds at their back.

Cavanaugh was well built in his day. You could see that right off; sturdy legs, and forearms the size of calves. His hands were thick from so many years of squeezing the blood from a baseball.

If Ray Cavanaugh said it once, he said it a thousand times, "If you're gonna give anything less than a hundred percent, you might as well quit." His ball club was made of players half as good, but who tried twice as hard. If you made his team you had a reason to be proud.

The team was dressed out and ready to take the field. We were just waiting for the word from Cavanaugh. The butterflies were panging in my stomach and Cavanaugh was still standing in the doorway tossing the baseball.

"How do you feel, Corey?" our catcher, Mike Posie asked.

"I feel pretty good," I said, and looked up to see if Cavanaugh was listening. There was no change in his rhythm.

"I saw the Anson County guys gettin' off the bus. Man, they're big as hell," Cole said.

"Yeah they are," Seth agreed.

"Must be the water," Cole said.

"How are you feeling, Roly?" Mike asked the other likely candidate to be throwing tonight.

"I feel good, man. Real loose," Roly replied.

"Let's go … It's game time," Coach Cavanaugh called out, as if he had just been summoned by a greater being to get this game underway. He tossed the ball in the air like a coin that would determine some mystical fate and quickly snagged it from thin air. I heard the loud pop as it hit hard in the palm of his hand. He tossed the game ball to me and said, "Make every pitch count tonight, son."

My thoughts teetered on that fine line that separates excitement from worry and anticipation from fear, and I immediately felt the pressure of a ball club's destiny resting on my shoulders.

Cavanaugh remained in the doorway as each man in turn filed past him. He inspected our uniforms and pointed out each player's weakness—the things we needed to do right tonight.

"I wanna see some hustle Manny … Hold up now. What is that?" Cavanaugh said, reaching out and grabbing the lobe of Manny's ear, stopping our center fielder in his tracks.

"It's my ear rings coach," Todd answered. He was trying to sneak by with a little glitter for the ladies in the stands. We could never figure out how he kept so many girlfriends. They even sat together at the games.

"Take 'em off," Cavanaugh said evenly, and Todd headed back to his locker deflated.

"Fitz, head up, butt down, come on son," he said to our all-conference short stop, Seth Fitz.

"Parker, I don't want to see any shenanigans tonight … no hot dogging out there," he said to our left fielder who had a reputation for showing off.

When all fourteen of us had filed past Cavanaugh, the tunnel was filled with the echoing sounds of hundreds of metal cleats scratching at the concrete. The light was dim, but shone bright at the end of the long corridor. In a booming voice that seemed to come from a distant mountain top or a deep valley Cavanaugh called out, "It's your night to shine!" His words echoed through the tunnel and were still ringing in our ears as we emerged onto the field.

The place was packed. It looked like everyone in Anson County had made the trip for the division championship. The newspapers had made a big deal about the series, as both teams had their entire rosters returning and last year's game had been an eleven inning epic, with Anson County on top. To add to the excitement, we had been given the opportunity to play in the recently built AAA stadium in our hometown of Fayetteville, North Carolina.

I was overwhelmed by the size of the stadium, the bright lights, and the hoards of people. We had never played in a real ballpark, but tonight we were kids living in a grown-up's world.

I bent down to tighten the laces on my cleats and the world stopped for one brief moment. I smelled the freshly cut grass, noted the perfect symmetry of the infield, the bases that looked like white islands in a sea of red clay, a sprawling outfield that rolled on forever, and a wall built for giants surrounding it all—420 feet to dead center. The place was huge.

In my hand was the game ball, not a dimple or cut in the leather, but perfectly smooth. The red laces were bright against the white. The ball felt small in my hand, and as familiar as anything I had ever touched. I love this game, I thought to myself, and the feeling had never been stronger.

"Get two," a strong voice bellowed out across the field, as a loud crack sounded and a baseball moved as a blur across the infield. The Anson County shortstop snagged the hot grounder and rifled it to the first baseman, who in turn rifled it home.

"Damn, they look pretty good," Cole said.

We stood wide-eyed in amazement as Anson County took their infield warm-ups, and I realized why Coach Cavanaugh always said it was important to make an impression on your adversaries before the game. We were nervous now.

When Anson County was finished, we took the field.

"First base," Cavanaugh yelled, and sent a shell down the third base line toward Frank Roystone. Stoney, the nickname he went by, flagged it down and made a crisp throw to first base. I heard the unmistakable "damn," that was Cole's comment of being impressed, and saw the first set of smiles ripple across the faces of my teammates. Our first baseman, Rod Godfrey, pointed and waved his gloved hand at Stoney in recognition of his prowess as our third baseman.

Everyone was breathing easier now. We were in the spotlight after such an impressive display from the Anson County Tigers, but we were just as comfortable at our positions as they were at theirs.

"All right, you can get down now," I said to the second string catcher and started my warm-ups. I imagined I was on the mound at game time, moving the ball around the plate, inside corner, outside corner, low in the strike zone, high and tight, as if a batter were in the box. I was relieved at how I was throwing despite the butterflies in my stomach.

"Lookin' good, son," my father said, coming towards the bull pen. I turned and saw him standing there wearing a worn Baltimore Oriole's baseball cap.

"How do you feel tonight?" he asked.

"Good. Really good. I'm throwin' hard," I replied.

"Mix it up. They're good hitters. Just that fastball isn't enough," he reminded me.

I moved my cap up and down on my head, scratching

my forehead with the inseam. It was a nervous habit of mine.

I walked over to the fence and stood looking up at my father; the man my friends and I called the giant. He was a massive man, standing 6'4" and built solid as a wall.

"About last night, Dad. Are you mad at me too?" I asked, referring to the yelling match between me and my mother the night before.

"Not mad, just disappointed. But don't worry about that now. Just concentrate on the game," he said, looking out across the field. "Your mother will come around. It'll just take some more time."

His tone became distant as his eyes left mine. The words had been spoken mechanically and without a thought. They were just words, the same ones he always used: 'Just give her some time.' My father wasn't one to intervene. His way was to just let things work themselves out.

"Watch out for number sixteen," my father said, referring to the Anson County first baseman who was the best hitter in the conference. "Don't be afraid to throw him inside."

"Yes sir," I replied, and went back to my warm-ups.

Chapter 5

"**L**ADIES AND GENTLEMEN, all rise for the singing of the National Anthem," crackled through the speakers. Our team and theirs stood shoulder to shoulder down the base paths as the words of the Star Spangled Banner echoed through the stadium.

'O'er the land of the free, and the home of the Braaave' … the crowd cheered, we donned our caps and took the field. It was a feeling that never lost its appeal or its excitement: desire to do your best as an individual and to win as a team.

I took the mound and Mike crouched down behind the plate. I dug out some dirt around the rubber so my foot would turn better in the hole. The mound was much steeper than the one on our home field and the steepness added some extra velocity to my fastball. KaPow. KaPow. KaPow. My fastballs were striking the sweet spot in Mike's catcher's mitt like a golfer on the driving range whose clubs keep striking perfectly. Mike couldn't get the ball back to me fast enough.

The chatter in the dugout of the Anson County Tigers died down as I continued my warm-ups. When I felt loose I signaled to Mike that I was ready. He and the infielders congregated at the mound.

I stood on a baseball mound with the best friends I would ever know and teammates for as long as I could remember and realized that tonight was a really big night. I saw the same thing in their eyes that was in mine: fear that our dream would end here. Each man in the huddle placed a hand in, we pushed down in unison, and took our positions.

"Batter up," the umpire yelled, pulled his mask down and assumed his kneeling position behind Mike. The Anson County batter took his stance: bat back, hands slightly out in front, left shoulder tucked down and eyes looking straight at me.

Mike signaled for a curveball by dropping two fingers down between his legs. It was a game we played with the opponent's first base coach. Mike would flash great big bunny ears with his fingers, like he was a rookie catcher who didn't know any better than to cover up his signals. Then we would wait for the base coach to shout out something about a curveball, thinking he had stolen the signal.

"Yeah right," I said under my breath as I spread my fingers wide across the seams for a fastball. I had started and ended every game with a heater and Mike had caught every one of them.

"Watch for the curve, Tommy," the Anson County third base coach called out on cue.

"Let's see what this guy's got, Corey," Mike said,

punched his glove and settled down on his knees.

I delivered a fastball with all I had. The batter took a massive cut, but came up short.

"That's what I thought he had," Mike chided, snapping the ball back to me.

The batter turned and looked down at Mike and kicked up some dirt. Mike shot him a wide grin through the catcher's mask and said, "Let's play ball."

By the ninth inning Manny had stolen four bases and crossed home plate three times, giving us a 3-2 lead. I had given up only three base hits, walked three batters, and had eleven strikeouts. Seth was setting the place on fire with his bat, four for four with two doubles, and put on quite a display of agility in the field. I believe nerves got the better of Cole, as he was no more than a sleeping giant.

When I took the mound for the last inning, I was facing the top of their line-up with just a one run lead.

"Strike this guy out Corey. I don't like the way he walks," Cole said, as the Anson County short stop strutted up to the plate.

There was a lot of chatter from the stands, from the field, and from both dugouts. We were at the point in the game where sheer determination can make you or break you, and both teams had a lot to lose. There wouldn't be any you'll-get-'em-next-time speeches in the locker room; this was it, winner takes all. It seemed like my whole childhood and my entire high school baseball career was being summed up in just three outs.

I reached deep for everything I had and the next string of pitches were some of the best I ever threw. I struck out the side. My team mates almost knocked me off the mound, and Mike placed the game ball in my glove, saying, "This one's for you."

The Hillcrest Bulldogs were on their way to the state playoffs.

Our celebration on the mound was brief but intense. Cavanaugh had warned us about gloating in front of a defeated opponent, so we shook hands with the Anson County Tigers and retired to the dugout.

"Sure, I'll get him," I heard Coach Cavanaugh say to someone through the fence. "Wails, someone out here to talk to you."

I walked around the fence and saw a man standing there wearing a black Cleveland Indian's jacket, carrying a clipboard in his hand. He must have been a foot taller than me and twice as wide.

"I'm John Littleman," the big man said. I thought the name was ironic, and was certain he must have heard what I wanted to say at least a million times, so I didn't say it.

"I'm a pitching scout for the Cleveland Indians," he continued.

"Oh yeah," I answered.

"I like the way you threw the ball tonight, son."

"Thank you."

"You keep pitching like that and we may have something to talk about when the playoffs are over," Littleman said in a deep voice.

He handed me a business card and told me to give it to my father. "Have him call my office next week," Littleman said. As he walked away I knew my dreams were on his clipboard.

Another group of men, also wearing university jackets

and carrying clipboards were walking past me.

"You talkin' about Fitz," the biggest man said.

"Yeah, what d'ya think, Ernie?" another one replied.

"Good ball player. Real solid in the field, and a pretty good stick tonight," another man answered.

"I thought that O'Conner kid was supposed to be something else?"

"Didn't impress me," the fat one replied.

I noticed a different group of men talking to Todd Manny behind the dugout. Todd was grinning ear to ear. I knew no matter what they were saying to him, his mind was on the girls.

I saw my father coming towards me. He was walking with Emily's dad, and both were grinning.

"You pitched a good ball game son," my father said, as we shook hands vigorously. "You could stand a little batting practice," he added.

"Well deserved, Corey. You made a fine showing tonight," Mr. Vallent said.

"Thank you Mr. Vallent," I replied.

Emily was right behind my father, and Royal was tagging along at her heels. She gave me a big hug and a small kiss on my cheek before her mother walked up.

"What did the big guy want, Corey?" my father asked, and I handed him the business card.

"Way to go Corey," Emily said. "You were great out there tonight. And how about Seth? All the scouts were talking about him."

Mr. Vallent peered over my father's shoulder and read the words on the card. Cleveland Indians was written across the top.

"I told you Robert—I heard that big guy talking about Corey. Might be some opportunity there," Mr. Vallent said.

"Corey needs whatever he's selling about like he needs a hole in his head," my father said.

I don't know what it was about pro baseball scouts, but my father didn't like them one bit. He said they would ruin my life. My father was a firm believer in education above all else.

Royal was begging for my attention, so I knelt down and rubbed his neck.

"I thought Linda would be here tonight," Mrs. Vallent said inquisitively, looking at my father for an answer.

She knew my mother didn't come to baseball games, and I wondered what made her say such a thing now. Mrs. Vallent was standing behind Emily with her hands draped over her daughter's shoulders. The two looked more like sisters than mother and daughter. Maybe it was the matching ribbons in their hair.

"Maybe next one," my father replied without hesitation.

"One of these nights there isn't going to be a next one," Mrs. Vallent said, raising her glance.

Our family may not have been as good as others at hiding our troubles, but we certainly weren't going to air them out here. Only flies on the wall know how many times the question was asked, 'why doesn't Corey's mother ever come watch her son play baseball?'

It was the same thing after every game. I watched my teammates mingling with their families, and I thought about my own. There was a time when I looked for my mother in the stands. I thought if I played better, she would come. If I had my name in the paper, she would be there. If I made the all-star team, she would take the time to watch. I accomplished all those things and still I played for only my father and myself.

My mother knew I could run to the baseball field and hide there, but when the stadium lights went out and the field was locked and there was nowhere else to hide, she would have dominion over all that remained—everything except a baseball diamond.

Chapter 6

AFTER THE GAME I took the bus back to the school with the team. You would have thought we had just won the World Series—the smiles, the laughing, the chatter, and the excitement was insurmountable. Manny led the hurrahs with his bigger than life grin and charisma. Posie was the most jovial about the win, telling us stories about some of the words exchanged between him and the batters; him doing the egging and their curt remarks, all of them ending with Posie saying, "What's the scoreboard say, buddy." We told stories and reveled in our accomplishment all the way back to the school. We unloaded the bus, complimented each other on the win one last time, and headed home.

When I pulled into the drive way I noticed my father walking around the yard moving his network of sprinklers here and there so the perfect amount of moisture would be paid-out in all the right places. When he saw me getting out of my jeep, he called out:

"Sure wish you guys had done that last year. It was a close ball game but there was never a doubt about who was the best team this year."

"No sir. It was a solid win," I replied.

Royal heard my voice, abandoned my father and came running to my side. I rubbed behind his ears and asked him what he done with his day.

"I'll tell you what he did—looks like he spent most of it digging up rabbits in my yard," my father said, put off.

I noticed Royal was covered in a thin layer of sandy, light soil, so there was no taking up for him. I apologized for his bad manners and headed into the house for some dinner.

"I told you not to leave that dog of yours alone for so long—he hasn't stopped howling all night. Where have you been anyway?" my mother said in a tone mixed of scorn and derision.

"We had a game tonight, in case you didn't know," I replied with enough disdain to infuriate the Pope. "You see my uniform don't you?"

"Don't get smart with me young man," she replied.

I shrugged it off and went straight to the refrigerator for something to eat. She stepped into the kitchen, and I could feel her cold stare on my back.

"Didn't I tell you not to wear those cleats in this kitchen? They ruin the floor."

I made no reply. It was best to keep my mouth shut.

"Do you hear me? I'm talking to you," she said louder this time.

I found a container of left-over spaghetti, took it out, and turned toward the microwave. My mother was infuriated; I could see it in her eyes and in her posture, the way she stood with her hands on her hips in an ominous pose of strength and superiority. I no longer wondered about her or what made her act this way. I was used to it by now, and did my part to fuel it. Why not, I often thought.

She asked me a third time if I heard her. I mumbled, 'so what,' under my breath.

With much more agility than I thought she was capable, she closed the distance between us in an instant and struck me with a wooden spoon.

Whack. Whack.

I dropped to my knees and covered my head. The third blow struck my knuckles.

"Don't you ever talk to me like that again. Do you hear me? You ungrateful brat." Her lips were pursed and her hands were trembling. Her eyes were red with fury and dark with disgust.

"I'm sorry … jeeez. I don't know what the problem is. Why are you so mad?" I said, trying to back pedal my way out.

"I'll tell you what the problem is. You walk around here like you don't care about anybody or anything—you and that dog. You leave everything a mess, you don't say anything to anyone. Who do you think you are?"

"I don't …"

"I don't know, I don't know," she mocked me. "Is that all you can say? Well I'll tell you this—you'd better find out and soon. You little brat. I'll bet you think twice after your father gets a hold of you," my mother yelled in a tone of puerility, turned and stormed out of the kitchen. A moment later she slammed her bedroom door so violently I knew it must be hanging from the hinges.

Her yelling was loud enough for my father to hear, and in case it was not, the door slamming certainly was. She was the hot-headed one, but her intemperance was never satisfied until my father was involved. She strove and strove to wear me down; to wear me down to nothing, until the day I would march along beside her taking her orders diligently. To break prison bars with my bare hands would have been easier than to learn the secrets that made my mother such a menace. I was certain of it.

It was the sound of my father's heaviness entering the house that instilled the fear in me my mother lacked with a wooden spoon.

"What's going on in here? What did you say to your mother?" my father asked as he entered the kitchen. He didn't play charades like my mother; with him it was all business.

"I didn't say anything," I answered meekly, still sitting on the floor.

My mother came back to the kitchen screaming. She had stomped down the hall and slammed the door simply for effect, and returned as soon as her act was complete.

"You didn't say anything … you didn't say anything," she yelled in disbelief. "I can not believe you. You are going to sit there and lie to your father like that?"

"Linda, what in the world is going on?" my father asked, once again the judge and jury in a trial between his wife and son.

"That little brat said, 'so what' to me," she protested, mocking me in a repulsive tone that made 'so what' sound worse than when I said it.

"Stand up," my father said evenly. "Did you say that to your mother?"

"Of course he said it Robert. Do you think I made it up?" my mother replied, turning her glare towards my father.

I just wanted to be gone, to a place where the yelling and

fighting never went on, and away from this crazy woman. I wanted out of the whole mess, but more than any other feeling I was scared. I was scared because of the look in my father's eyes. It was worse with him. My mother was crazy and irrational, but my father was controlled and deliberate, and the look in his eyes scared me. He was thinking, reenacting in his mind my words, "so what." She left him to punish me for something that was between me and her. It was a cheap escape and a pathetic act, and both created nothing but malice between us. No matter what he did to me, I would consider it her.

I was looking up at my father, worried, anxious for a verdict, sullen with fear, when I noticed my mother in the doorway. The slight creases at the corners of her mouth, a widening grin, and a derisive smile were all telling of her victory over me.

My father moved quickly. When I saw his hand come up, I turned my shoulder and ducked my head. He grabbed me by the back of the neck and squeezed until my knees buckled. Through gritted teeth he said, "Son, if you ever say something like that to your mother again, I swear you will regret it. Now go to your room."

On the way to my room I saw Royal sitting in the middle of the yard staring at the kitchen window. I walked onto the deck and called out to him. "It's OK boy. Go back to sleep," I said reassuringly. He wagged his tail at the sound of my voice.

I went to my room like my father told me, laid down on my bed and stared at the ceiling. Gritting my teeth and clinching my fists, I thought of how much I despised that woman. I pondered a better life than the one I was a part of here. She must be the most miserable person on Earth, I thought. If I combed the world I could never find another person so distraught and so afflicted.

My bedroom door opened and my father walked in.

"Son, you have got to stop this," he said beseechingly, begging for mercy.

"Dad, she's crazy. You don't understand. What the hell is wrong ..."

"Listen to me, Corey. I do understand, but you are not going to win. I'm just telling you—you're not. If you keep this up your mother is going to leave, and I don't want that. I want you to be polite. I want you to do what she tells you, when she tells you."

I was looking at the floor and not paying attention to my father. I may have been a kid in his eyes, but I was old enough to know the meaning of the word fair and I wasn't getting it.

My father grabbed my jaw and forced my eyes to meet his. "Do you understand me, Corey?"

I nodded not of approval, but of having heard his words.

"You don't want me to get involved," my father said sternly. His emphasis on 'don't' was overkill, as his intimidation needed no assistance. "You and your mother need to work this out," he said, and left me to my thoughts.

'Work it out with your mother,' he says to me. Yeah right. I could grow wings and fly away just as easily. We could not stand to be in the same room together; the house was not big enough for the two of us; I doubted if the entire city was a large enough place for the two of us to coexist peacefully.

It must be me, I thought; it must be the sight of me that

infuriates her. When my mother looks at me she must see the freedom she passed up to have a son, and that son has been a waste of time. I thought about Royal and remembered the day I got him. He was a present from her so there was a time when she didn't hate me, but her coldness is as complete as a frozen pond, I thought, only it stops at the water's edge. She is only this way with me, but a wonderful, charming person to the community. She uses up any kindness she possesses on the audience and leaves me with the crap that remains. My stomach knotted in disgust. I knew the real Linda Wails and everyone else was fooled by an actress playing her part.

Chapter 7

MY MIND REMEMBERS easily the very good and the very bad; mediocrity lies somewhere in between and is mostly forgotten.

From a small farming town in Northern Virginia came a gem that shone brighter than most. Linda Wails stood a head taller than other women. Her shoulders were broad and strong. Her complexion was flawless. Her hair was a mixture of brown and amber, wavy and unkempt, flowing down her back. Her eyes were dark, her cheekbones high and angled, and her neck slender. She possessed raw beauty and raw strength. To be certain, my mother stood out in a crowd.

My grandmother said she was a pill. My grandfather said she was the cat's meow. Lucky for my father he found Linda before the world had a chance to find her. They were married on the family farm in Warrenton, Virginia when my mother was 19. Some say that was her problem—she married too young.

My father having been the son of a farmer himself despised the occupation. He thought farming was an idle job, requiring little use of his mind. He received an academic scholarship to the University of Maryland, and in 1973 he began earning his degree in Aeronautical Space Engineering, an unlikely endeavor for a farm boy from Culpeper. Some say he had a lot to prove.

Four years later my father graduated from college and went looking for a job. But where were aeronautical space engineering jobs in 1974? Seattle, Washington, the home of Boeing Industries. My mother flat-out refused to move and for the next three years my father drove a Sunbeam bread truck in rural Virginia. His territory was from Manassas to Opal. How ridiculous he must have felt wearing a sunbeam bread uniform with a Space Engineering degree in his back pocket. Of course, farming was an option, but Robert Wails said it a million times: he had bailed enough hay in his lifetime.

My mother was content living a quiet life, two miles from her parent's home on the farm. Everything that was important to her was within her grasp: her parents, her husband, and her son. To her I owe a great childhood. I remember …

The Blue Ridge Mountains on the horizon silhouetted by a low angle sun; My Grandfather called it daybreak, I called it sunrise. Whatever the name it was beautiful. The cold from the night rushing toward the sky, the bottom lands covered in a haze of dew, the clouds parting ways exposing the mountains, and everything was rising.

When the white bee boxes were painted with gold rays, we headed into the forest. The bees were busy gathering pollen and nectar. Winter was over and summer on the make. The bees knew better than anyone, and white honey was waiting for the taking.

The old man opened the hives carefully, and the sky filled with God's diligent creatures. Sycamores, Southern Oaks, and Tulip Poplars lined the trail out of the woods, and a breeze had them dancing together.

I can remember a day I thought would never end; a place, a time, and a family that would last forever. If ignorance is bliss then childhood is heaven itself.

My grandfather's death was unexpected and improbable, but it happened just the same. He had a heat stroke and fell from the roof of the barn. For what it's worth, the emergency crew said he would have survived the stroke—the fall was a different story. Why they bothered to tell us such a thing is beyond me.

His death marked the end of my childhood. I was eight years old when I learned that things don't stay the same forever. I was young and resilient, but my mother never did recover. His death exposed a loose thread, and her whole life began to unravel.

My grandmother, in an effort to keep the family farm, leased most of the land to a tenant farmer. We filled in and did the rest of the work, but it was an all uphill battle.

Two years later my parents were forced to sell the land. The taxes alone were more than the profits. We moved my grandmother to a house in the city, and my father took a job as an industrial engineer for Goodyear Tire Company. That job took our family to Fayetteville, North Carolina, where his career finally got underway.

My mother didn't fair very well in Fayetteville. She

complained incessantly about all the things she hated about her new life. She blamed my father for moving her to such a god forsaken place, a place so drastically different from the farm.

When I was young it was from her I learned not to harp on things you can't change, and I wondered why she was not living by her own advice. Maybe her father's death was the first in a series of things outside of her control.

As for me, I played baseball day in and day out. Even in the winter I practiced indoors. I was happy in North Carolina. I made great friends with Cole and Seth, and I was in love with Emily Vallent. I missed the way things used to be, but it wasn't something I could change.

Chapter 8

THE TEAM did not have official baseball practice on Sundays and Cavanaugh gave us Saturday off, so we planned a camping trip to one of our favorite camping spots, Raven's Rock.

On Saturday morning, bright and early, my mother saw me loading up my jeep and asked where I thought I was going. I told her we were going camping. Royal was already in the jeep ready to go.

"You're not going anywhere," she replied, matter of fact.

"Why not?" I asked.

"You've got work to do. You're gonna clean out the shed, pick up after your dog, and straighten up your room. You just call your friends and tell them you aren't going anywhere." Linda Wails had spoken.

"Mom, come on," I pleaded. "We've had this camping trip planned for two weeks. I can do that on Sunday. I'll come back early. I promise."

"*I promise*," she mocked me. "No. You'll do it now," she said, and walked back into the house.

There comes a time when enough is enough and I thought maybe today was the day. Today was the day when I would say the hell with it and do whatever I wanted. My rational self kicked me in the side and told me I had three more months until graduation, and I had to stick it out. Running away was out of the question.

"Corey! Get in here," my mother yelled from the kitchen.

"Did you do this?" she said, holding up a silver pan whose inside was black where I had burned clam chowder. I had tried to get the stain off but it was permanent. Things were getting worse. I could see that right off.

"Yes Ma'am. I was making clam chowder …" I started, but stopped to catch the pan that was coming at me.

"It's just a pan, Mom," I said in a pliable voice, hoping to get out of this with the least amount of injury possible.

"*It's just a pan, Mom*," she sneered. More than anything, I hated the way she mocked me. I wanted to tape record her and play it back so she could hear how ridiculous she sounded, like a little kid.

"Did you buy that pan?" she continued.

I made no answer. Shutting up was the best thing to do now. I never should have said a word to begin with. I knew better. Any word I said always came back in her sarcastic tone like a parrot.

"Well did you?" she asked again.

"No, I didn't buy the pan," I said, exhausted. I felt like telling her about the unbelievable flush of déjà vu that rippled through my brain; haven't we had this argument a thousand times, I thought to myself. I didn't dare smile out loud, but I was thinking about it.

"Don't tell me It's just a pan then. I know what it is. I paid twenty dollars for it, and it's ruined. Go throw it away."

I decided I had gotten out easy as I tossed the pan in the dumpster on my way to the shed. I called Royal and he jumped out of the jeep and followed me up the hill.

He had a good time inspecting all the things I pulled out of the shed and laid on the ground. He would not have been having so much fun if he knew this mundane task was instead of a camping trip. The beauty of being a dog, I thought, he has no idea what he is missing.

Seth, Jake, and Cole pulled up out front at one o'clock. I heard my mother greet them on the back porch.

"Hey Mrs. Wails. Where's Corey?" Cole asked.

"He's out back, working in the shed. I told him months ago that he needed to get it cleaned up. If he finishes, maybe he can go with you boys," my mother said politely, in the softest voice she could muster.

I couldn't stand to hear her tell lies to my friends. There was no chance I was getting out of here today, and she knew it. Even if I did finish this task, she would have another one waiting for me.

The guys walked back to where I was working and asked what I was doing. Cole laughed, watching me lay a weed-eater on the ground, next to a shovel, and a leaf blower. Jake and Seth played with Royal, and for a minute I thought about letting them take him to Raven's Rock. It didn't seem fair that he was trapped too, but I decided I couldn't do this alone, so he would have to stay.

"Man, I can't go. She's got all kinds of things for me to do," I said.

"Do it tomorrow. We'll come back early," Seth suggested.

"I already offered that. She said no," I answered.

"If we help, we can finish this up in no time," Cole said.

"Don't listen to her. She isn't gonna let me go no matter what. It's not about the shed anyway. If I go camping, she won't have anyone to yell at," I answered.

"Let's get this done, and I'll tell her you're finished. She'll let you go. She told me so," Cole said.

The four of us cleaned the shed top to bottom. We cleared away all the cob webs, swept the floors, wiped off the yard tools, and put everything back inside neatly. Less than an hour later Cole ambled off to the house to get my mother for an inspection.

I was trying to look sharp when my mother returned with Cole. I was going the extra yard by wiping down the lawn mower engine with a rag. My mother had a terrible look on her face, like she had been bested by a couple of teenagers.

"There it is Mrs. Wails. Clean as a whistle," Cole said, and I knew for sure his attitude alone would get me in trouble. He didn't know her like I did.

She looked things over for a brief second, shot me a glare, and said, "It looks good boys. I want the dishwasher unloaded, Corey, and then you can go." With that, she turned and walked back to the house.

She was one heck of a good actress. Her smile lit up the whole yard. But I knew I wouldn't get out that easy.

We all headed into the kitchen to finish the last task of the day, and off to Raven's Rock. I was excited beyond repair. In the back of my mind I wondered why things had to be this way; to have to play all these games just to go on a camping trip for one night. You would think I was asking for a new car.

The guys found something to eat and I was putting the dishes away. My mother was standing beside me at the sink, washing the pots and pans by hand. I grabbed a measuring cup and thought about where it went. I didn't know for sure, but it was glass, so I figured I would put it with the other glasses. I was incorrect, and was made well aware of my blunder. Whack. She clocked me on the back of the head with something.

I was much bolder with my friends in the room, and I felt like a pansy taking her abuse without a fight.

"What the hell is your problem?" I said, instantly turning to face her. I noticed a large mixing spoon in her hand.

She made no reply. We stood there, eyes locked, adversaries with no respect for one another. She tried to hit me again, only I moved. I looked at her with a feeling of satisfaction; satisfied for not taking her crap willingly, not in front of my friends.

"Go to your room!" she screamed, infuriated. Her voice cracked along with her control.

"No. You said I could go camping and that's where I'm going."

She put the spoon down and slapped me across the face. I could have ducked, or blocked it, but I let her have it, because it was going to be the last time. Maybe the feeling of her hand on my skin would be the harsh reality she needed to feel her own malignancy. She was no longer fit to be anyone's mother.

Chapter 9

WHEN LINDA WAILS was involved there was a price to pay for everything, and I knew that price would be high for blatantly disrespecting her in front of my friends.

I enjoyed the camping trip to Raven's Rock as much as I could, but in the back of my mind I was worried, wondering if my father would get involved. I wondered if she would appeal to him the seriousness of my offense and demand repercussion. I did not want to tangle with my father; that was a fight I would lose. What I wondered about the most was why there had to be any fight at all? I didn't understand why we couldn't get along.

Sunday came too quickly and I found myself in sight of my house. I was scared to go in, so I went to Emily's instead. I stayed there until midnight and then went home. I snuck in through the downstairs and put Royal in the yard, and as quietly as I could went to my room. I did not wake my parents, and was relieved when I put my head on the pillow and went to sleep.

I heard the door slam against the wall as she came. My

alarm clock was going off—Aaant, Aaant, Aaaant. I was half awake and half asleep.

"Get out of bed, you lazy shit," my mother screamed, snatching the covers off my bed and dragging them across the room on her way back to the bathroom.

Nothing like waking up in the morning to 'you lazy shit,' I thought, struggling with the morning clouds in my head. I heard the hair dryer, and knew she was just outside my bedroom in the bathroom. I reached over, silenced the alarm clock, and fell back asleep. It was the perfect time to sleep, cognizant enough to know that you are actually sleeping. In this state I could practically will my own dreams.

I was lying there, one ear on the hair dryer, ready to jump to my feet as soon as I heard it stop, the other intent on getting just a few more minutes of rest. I guess I took it a little too far, because I did not hear her come back.

Whack. Whack. Along with the twinge of pain came the sound of shattering glass. She hit me with her hand mirror square on my knee and the broken pieces went everywhere.

"I told you to get up. NOW!" my mother screamed, incensed at my laziness.

"I am. I am," I said, trying to get my wits about me and decipher what was going on. My mother was standing over me holding a broken mirror in her hand.

"Look at what you made me do," she said, her tone incredulous, as if it had not been her at all but someone else who shared her body.

"I didn't make you do anything but you're gonna get seven years of bad luck for it," I said, pushing the glass away and rubbing my knee. Her actions evaded me completely.

"NOW Corey! Get out of bed!" she screamed, waving the mirror.

"Jesus Christ, Mom. I'm getting up. What in the world is wrong with you?" I yelled.

"Oh you little brat," she said in an awful voice. "You know exactly what is wrong with me, and you don't care one bit. You don't care about anyone except yourself. I don't know how I ever raised such a selfish little brat." She turned and stormed out of my room.

Chapter 10

THE WAY THINGS WERE GOING at home I would never make it to graduation unless I stepped up my measures of avoidance. I went into stealth mode, sneaking around the house feeding Royal and myself, and the rest of the time I stayed away. After practice I went to either Emily's house or Cole's, and returned only in the mornings when my parents were gone.

One of those mornings, while I was in the kitchen making my breakfast, I noticed a brochure lying on the counter top. On the cover was the American Cancer Society emblem. The brochure was from the Duke Cancer Clinic. The sight of it brought back a lot of bad memories: my mother crying to my father about having breast cancer; the conversations I heard through the walls and had to put a pillow over my head to stop. I had never heard my mother cry like that, and it wasn't something I understood. The American Cancer Society logo said a lot without a single word. I picked up the flier and a parking ticket fell from the pamphlet. It was stamped with the previous day's date.

My father came by the baseball field and watched us practice from time to time, so I had seen him. He did not seem to have a problem with me staying away, and I could tell by his happy-go-lucky attitude that things were pleasant for a change. It upset me to know whose team he was on and reinforced my thoughts: my mother's derision was aimed only at me.

My father's take on life was to live and learn, and at seventeen years old, he figured I could make my own decisions, so he did not intervene. The entire affair, my mother, my father, my family and all of our troubles seemed to be an obstacle standing in the way of accomplishing my dreams. I tried to put it out of my head like a ball player who hears no chatter. I tightened my blinders and focused straight ahead. I could see the finish line and wanted to be there yesterday.

No one except Emily knew what I went through at home. It embarrassed me that I could not function in my own house, with my own mother, and I did not want anyone to know. Emily and I talked about it some; only because she brought it up and only until I could change the subject, which was hard with her.

One night at Emily's house when I was talking about leaving this place forever, she said to me, "I will never leave you, Corey Wails. I will be here when you come back, and I will always love you."

I am certain she had no idea how many times in my life I would play those words over and over in my head, knowing that no matter how alone I felt I would always have her.

I did not believe in love the way Emily did. She saw the emotion lasting a lifetime, a soft warm feeling that would never leave her heart, an emotion that grows with time and only gets stronger. She told me so, and she told me that love for her was me.

I believed something entirely different. It is to be avoided at all cost; an emotion I never understood until the thing I loved was gone, and then it hit me in the head like a ton of bricks, buckled my knees, and sent me to the ground. Love is something that hurts and something that doesn't last forever.

Emily and I talked about it, but I could never make her understand why we were so different. I loved my Grandfather, and he died. As a child, I loved my mother, but she changed. Here and now, I love Emily Vallent, but it will not last. This is the way I lived my life—with lactic acid in my muscles from running and blinders on my eyes scared to see what was next to me.

Chapter 11

"**W**AILS, TAKE OFF UNTIL I GET TIRED," Coach Cavanaugh yelled. It was routine—I ran and like Cavanaugh said, until he got tired of watching me go by. Strange that the one thing I should hate about pitching was running. The rest of the team took batting practice, fielded fly balls and grounders; they worked on base running, turning double plays, and fielding bunts. While I ran, the team actually played baseball.

After a couple hours Cavanaugh waved me in. "Line up behind the plate," he said to the team, and put a wad of tobacco the size of a baseball in his cheek.

One at a time we took off down the first baseline. Manny, Fitz, Miller, and O'Conner started the drill; the fastest players up front, and the slowest bringing up the rear. I was somewhere in the middle.

I rubbed the insides of my legs trying to shake off the fatigue from running laps for two hours.

"Get goin' Wails," Cavanaugh yelled and I took off. As I

rounded first base I saw Manny rounding third and knew I was already in trouble. When he passed me I would be out of the drill and running suicides along the fence. Suicides were the worst of all Cavanaugh's conditioning drills. Back and forth, back and forth, we sprinted, and every time the assistant coach blew the whistle, we turned, touched the ground and sprinted the other way. I always wondered if the school cooks knew how much of their food was wasted by Cavanaugh's suicides.

Sure enough, Manny passed me rounding third base, but not without a comment.

"You white boys are awfully slow," he said, grinning wide as he blew by me.

It didn't take long for Manny and Fitz to leave the entire team in their wake, and we were all running suicides along the fence watching them chase one another around the bases. It was an impressive display of speed by both.

After practice I remained on the field to talk to Cavanaugh. Royal took his normal position at my side as I entered the dugout.

"Coach, can I talk to you for a minute?" I asked.

"What's on your mind son?"

I had half of Cavanaugh's attention. The other half was still going over the playbook from last night's game. I wanted to ask him about taking more batting practice. It seemed to me that I ran enough, but I wasn't a very good hitter. I voiced my opinion, and waited for his reply. I received only a lackadaisical "And?"

"Well, I was wondering if I could take some batting practice like everyone else, or maybe I could stay after practice and take some cuts," I persisted.

A long period of silence followed and I was beginning to regret bringing it up. I guess if you cut right to the chase, I was criticizing his coaching. I gave up on a reply, and turned to walk away, sorry I had even mentioned it.

"Do you wanna be a pitcher son?" Cavanaugh asked.

"Of course I do," I answered emphatically, turning back around.

"Then you'll run," Cavanaugh said. "If I thought you would take care of your own conditioning off the field, then you could hit with the team, but you'll just go squeezin' it up with Suzee as soon as practice is over."

"Emily, Coach Cavanaugh. My girlfriend's name is Emily," I said, hesitantly correcting him.

"It's an expression, son. Emily, Suzee, Bobbi Joe, whatever."

Cavanaugh went back to the books, and I knew this conversation was over.

"Yes sir," I replied and started towards the locker room.

Before I reached the mound, Cavanaugh stepped out of the dugout and said, "If you wanna take some cuts grab a bat."

Coach Cavanaugh and I took batting practice, just the two of us, for the rest of the playoffs. It improved my hitting, but more importantly it gave me a few less hours to spend hiding.

I went to Emily's house after practice that night. She was sitting on the front porch waiting for me when I got there. I barely had time to sit down when she started a conversation about my mother.

"Corey, your mother called my house tonight. She said you have not been home in two weeks."

"Yeah, so what?" I said.

"So what? Corey, what in the world is wrong with you? I had no idea you had not been home. You don't stay here every night. Where else do you go?"

"I stay at Cole's house if I am not here," I answered.

"Corey, you need to go home," Emily said, point blank.

"Why should I?" I replied. "I don't see what difference it makes. In three months I'm leaving forever anyway."

"Because she's your mother Corey. It is not a baseball game—it doesn't just end."

"Have you ever hated your mother, Emily?"

"Of course not," she replied, as if it were the most ridiculous notion on Earth.

"Not even for a minute after you got in trouble for something?" I persisted, hoping Emily would feel the full weight of the implication.

"No. Never," Emily said. "I have never thought of hating my parents, Corey. It's not right. It's just not."

"That is why I don't want to go home. That is why I don't care anymore. I hate that woman. She is not my mother anyway. I remember the woman I used to love, but she's gone, and I can't change that."

"What are you talking about, Corey?"

"You know what I'm talking about. You remember how great she used to be. She used to come to my games. She used to take us to the pool. She even bought Royal for me. I look at her now, and just want to shake the hell out of her and tell her to wake up. It's me … I'm your son."

"Have you ever thought that it's not just her, maybe it's

you too," Emily said. "I have seen the way you act around her. You are not very nice Corey."

It was tearing me apart, and I could feel it. Too many things were coming to a head at the same time. Baseball was almost over. I was graduating from high school in three months. I was worried about what would happen with me and Emily, and I was scared that I would be all alone in the world.

"Corey, your mother wants to talk to you. She sounded upset, and she asked me to talk to you," Emily said in a soft voice, but keeping her distance.

She sat looking at me, watching me break, wondering how I could be this way. How I could abandon my family, seemingly so easily? She had no idea how hard it really was.

"Why can't you tell your mother what you just told me?" she continued. "You two can work this out Corey. Your mother is not the terrible person you think she is. For some reason you just want to believe that."

Emily continued to give me her opinion. I could tell by her tone that she had wanted to say that to me for a long time. She found the courage somewhere to stand up and put me in my place. Emily said to me what no one else dared.

"You don't know what you're talking about Emily," I said angrily and stood up to leave. "It's so easy to solve other people's problems, isn't it?"

"I'm just trying to help you Corey. That's all."

"Thanks, but I don't need it," I replied sharply on my way out.

I drove around for a while, thinking, wondering if I should go home and see what my mother had to say.

Chapter 12

IT WAS NINE O'CLOCK when I got home and every light in the house was on. I heard my mother and father talking in the kitchen. I thought about leaving but was certain they already heard me come in, so I stayed.

As I came into the kitchen, I saw my father leaning on the counter and my mother seated beside him. My mother was staring down at the counter top, and my father was looking straight at me. On his face was an expression I had never seen. He looked confused, and something else. Perhaps it was sadness. Robert Wails was never any of those things. He didn't know the meaning of confusion and he didn't have time to be sad. Something about the way he was looking at me led me to think there was something he wanted to say, but could not.

"Well, I'd better go take a look at those papers, Linda. I'll let you and Corey talk now. We can finish this up later," he said.

He bent down and gave her a kiss on the forehead, and

turned to leave the room. His actions were nothing out of the ordinary, but my mother's were. As he started away, she grabbed him by the arm. Very slowly, her fingers traced a path from his forearm to his wrist.

"Thank you, Robert. Thank you for everything," she said softly.

When my father left the room, my mother and I were in the kitchen alone. She too looked different. I had never seen her so relaxed and so pensive, as if the weight of the world had been lifted from her shoulders and for some strange reason she missed the burden.

"Corey, there's lasagna in the oven. It's probably still warm," she said in a pleasant voice.

I glanced up at her while I was making my plate. She was sitting as still as a statue, staring at the counter top with both hands on either side of her face holding her head up. It was not like her to sit around like this, I thought.

I made my plate and sat down at the bar next to her.

"Is it good?" she asked, taking a hand away from her cheek, exposing a red mark on her face. She had been sitting there a long time, I thought.

"Yes Ma'am. It's good," I answered, monotone.

We sat in silence as I ate. My goal was to make it through dinner without an explosion between us. There was no use for small talk; we had been through all of that over the years; talking just for the sake of talking was not going to solve our problems.

"Corey, I have something I would like to talk to you about," she said agreeably.

"EmHm," I replied.

"When you finish your supper can we go for a walk?"

It may have been the craziest thing I had ever heard—
my mother and I going for a walk. But I kept my thoughts
to myself. I had learned the best way to get around her
was to keep my mouth shut. Agreeing with whatever she
said was always best in the long run.

"All right," I answered.

I ate a few more bites of lasagna, but had lost my
appetite. Something very strange was going on in my house,
and I felt it the moment I walked in the door. I could feel
it, and see it in my mother's face.

"Are you not going to finish?" she asked.

"No. I'm done." I said.

"Then let's go for a walk. I have something I need to
talk to you about," she said softly.

I followed her out the side door and through the carport.
I was just along for the ride. I was not going to open my
mouth. I followed a half a step behind her and a little off
to the side. She turned in the direction of the dead end
street that led to the woods.

"Corey, will you give me your hand?" she said.

We took a few more steps before I decided to grant her
this request. She moved her hand around mine for a long
time. I couldn't tell if she was trying to find the place they
fit together comfortably, or if she was remembering what it
felt like to hold my hand when I was just a boy. The feeling
was strange, but soft, like a mother's touch should be.

"Corey, I have some bad news to tell you," she said
gently.

The difference between bad news to her and bad news
to me were as distant in meaning as China and Texas are
in miles. If she was going to tell me that she was leaving

I would be jumping up and down.

The neighborhood was quiet and dark. The sun had gone down hours earlier; the month was March and the weather was unseasonably warm. The air was so humid I could see it hanging from the sky. We walked half the distance of the street still holding hands before she spoke again.

"Your father and I went to Duke last week," she finally said, and another period of silence followed. With her prolonged introduction to the purpose of this walk, my thoughts were wandering. There were nine dirty gray birds sitting on the electrical wire—garden variety pests. One flew away and eight stayed put.

Her touch was obtrusive and puzzling to me. At this rate we are going to be here all night, I thought. We stopped just short of the end of the street, where the woods started. My mother turned towards me. My mind was racing with thoughts I did not dare voice. Whatever problem she has is no concern of mine, and I could not believe she was acting like I am a part of it. What could she possibly want from me?

I was staring into the woods wondering if my old bike trail was still there when she finally got the nerve to tell me the purpose of this outing.

"Corey, the doctors told me that I have cancer again," she said.

"And," I replied.

"They told me I have it everywhere and it's a type that doesn't respond to treatment."

"What does that mean?" I asked, my tone callous.

"It means I'm going to die, Corey."

I looked back into the woods. I was no stranger to the pain of losing someone. I loved my Grandfather and hated that he died, but the woman in front of me I hardly knew. I had nothing to say and felt very little inside. It was her, not me, that made our life a game, and with this news she was simply advancing a pawn. Is she calling for an armistice because she is sick? If so, it will not be that easy. After all, she taught me how to play this game; she ought to know how good I am at it.

"Lots of people have cancer. You can do radiation and all of that ...same thing you did last time," I said, trying to devalue the worth of her bad news. She squeezed my hands tightly, stopping my thoughts.

"Corey, we need to work through this together. OK?" she said.

Her eyes were pleading. She was asking for something from me, perhaps for the first time ever. I realized one thing, and I realized it as soon as I looked into her begging eyes. She had lost her control over me. It was a day I will never forget and one I struggle to remember.

I agreed, or rather, I answered yes to her request and threw it to the back of my mind, filed away behind baseball games, homework assignments, and dreams of a better life than this one.

We walked back to the house in silence. My mother continued to hold and caress my hand all the way to the door. She let go of my hand just as we entered the house and her fingers lingered the way they had with my father earlier. I had never seen her this way. I had never seen her act as if she needed anything from anyone, but she wanted something from me and I had no idea what.

She stopped in the kitchen and started to clean up my dishes. As I was leaving the room, she turned from the sink to face me and I saw tears in her eyes. I was looking at the same person I resented more than anyone or anything in my life, but I was seeing a scared little girl, lips quivering with fear. The kind of fear only children know heading into the unknown.

"Give me a hug?" she said softly, with the intonation of a question. She stepped closer, and put her arms around me. When she pulled me close, I felt her body trembling. I was tall for my age, but still an inch shorter than she, allowing my chin to rest comfortably on her shoulder; my cheek pressed against her neck. She held me the way she had held my hand during our walk, as if she never wanted to let go. Many years had passed since I had been hugged by this woman, and even longer since I wanted to be. It was not something I thought would ever happen again, and it was not something I thought I missed. She loosened her hold and held me at arm's length.

"Corey, I want you to do me a favor," she said.

"Yes Ma'am?" I replied.

"I want you to think about what I asked you to-night?" she said. "About you and I working through this together."

She was in control of her emotions, but just barely. I could tell that every word was a struggle, and every thought was leading to another, deeper and deeper into an endless well of memories. Her eyes told me that she had much more to say. Her silence told me she had no right to say it.

I struggled with the complexity of her request. Did

she mean that now, all of a sudden, just like that, we were supposed to act like a mother and a son? The radical news she received, which was obviously affecting her tremendously, was her life, not mine. Was she asking me to forgive her and to forget years of resentment? That would be a hard task for a seventeen year old kid. I didn't know if I had the time and energy for what she was asking, and I certainly lacked the desire. If we were a baseball team Cavanaugh would cut me because my heart was not in the game.

"All right," I said. Agreeing with her was a habit, the path of least resistance, so I agreed once more, just so I could leave the room.

When I reached the other side of the living room, I stopped and looked back. There was space between the counter and the cabinets where I could see into the kitchen. All the lights were off except a dim lamp above the sink. The water was running, only she was not washing dishes. I could see her slouched shoulders and one hand on the counter top supporting her weight. She was not always as solid as a rock, I thought. She had only led me to believe so for all these years.

Chapter 13

THE NEXT MORNING Emily was waiting for me at the door of my first class. Cole spotted her first.

"Looks like someone wants to talk to you," Cole said. "Uh oh, trouble in paradise. I've seen that look before."

"Emily and I don't play those games. She's not mad at me."

"Yeah sure, Corey. I'll remind you of that when you're looking for a date for graduation."

Emily heard us coming down the hall and glanced up.

"Knock it off," I said to Cole, who drew an imaginary zipper across his lips. Emily had not heard him, but she saw his gesture.

"Hey Emily," Cole said and winked at my girlfriend. "I don't have a date to graduation. Just in case ..."

"No thanks, Cole, but I'll keep it in mind," Emily replied sarcastically.

Cole headed into class and I stayed in the hallway to talk to Emily.

"What's up, Em?" I asked.

"What was that all about?" she replied.

"Oh … just Cole being Cole," I said. "If you ever go out with him I think I'll jump off a bridge."

Emily laughed and I knew immediately that she wasn't mad at me. Her smile put things at ease.

"Why are you waiting for me?" I asked.

"I was worried about you last night. I'm sorry for some of the things I said. I didn't mean to upset you," she said.

"Em, it's not your fault. It never is. You don't have to apologize to me. I knew what you were getting at, and you're probably right in a lot of ways."

When the school late buzzer rang, there was Mr. Torant coming around the corner. I looked through the doorway of my classroom and saw Mr. Stewart sitting at his desk sipping on his coffee. He was looking at me and Emily.

"You better get in here before Mr. Torant sees you, boy," Mr. Stewart said.

"It's too late," I replied.

"Corey Wails, straight to my office … on the double," Mr. Torant called out in a harsh tone. "Emily, dear, you need to be in class. That was the late buzzer, you know," he said politely.

"Yes sir," Emily replied. She looked at me with her big, blue eyes smiling, and whispered, "What is it with you two?"

She hurried off down the hall and I started towards the office.

John Torant was seated behind his desk when I entered his office. He had rushed back to allow himself some time to pull my file.

"Mr. Wails," he said slowly, accentuating my last name. "Have a seat there," he continued, and pointed to the arm chair in front of his desk.

"You know son, school is a system, and here at Hillcrest that system begins at precisely 8:10 AM. If you can't follow the rules on your own, it's my job to help you. Rules are made for everyone, no exceptions."

"Then let's go get Emily," I quipped. I had a good point, but I should have hidden my smirk.

"Do you think this is funny, son? Do you think sitting in the vice principal's office is funny? Look around you—doesn't it strike you as odd that you're the only one here. Everyone else is in class, where they're supposed to be. But not you. Why? Because you choose not to follow the rules."

"Let's see," he said, looking at the chart he had pulled from the folder with my name on it. He ran his finger down the page and counted up the entries.

"Sixteen tardies. I could suspend you for this. Do you know what that means, Corey?"

"Yes sir," I replied, and straightened up in my chair; suspension would mean no more baseball.

"Oh, I've your attention now. Is that what it takes with you? If there's nothing for you to gain, then you don't want to participate. Is that it? If I suspend you, you can't play baseball," Mr. Torant said. "You understand that rule don't you?"

"Yes sir. I do."

"Let me tell you something, Corey. You may think I'm some mean ogre that has nothing better to do than to chase you down, stay on you all the time, as the saying goes—to ride your ass, but that's not it at all. It's my job to prepare you for the real world. The real world has rules, it has a system, and you have no choice but to follow them. Something as simple as getting here on time doesn't seem like too much to ask. Does it?"

"No sir. I guess not," I replied.

"What do your parents say about all of this?" Mr. Torant asked, leaning back in his chair.

"About all of what?" I replied.

"About you having been to my office sixteen times this year?"

"They don't know."

"Well maybe they should," Torant said quickly.

"Maybe."

"You're a real smart ass, aren't you Corey?" Mr. Torant said. "A real hum dinger of a hot shot."

"I don't mean to be," I replied.

Mr. Torant leaned forward on his elbows and looked straight at me. "Here's the deal, Corey. I LET you play baseball. That is what I do for you. Since you strike me as the kind of kid that only does something if he gets something in return, I'll make you a deal—you come to school on time and I will continue to let you play baseball. The next time you are late, you're off the team."

At the last class of the day, I took my seat next to Emily. I hadn't seen her since my run in with Mr. Torant. I could tell she was anxious to pick up our conversation where we left off.

"What did Mr. Torant say to you?" Emily asked.

"He says if I'm late one more time, I'm off the baseball

team."

"He can't do that," she exclaimed.

"Apparently he can. He gave me a big lecture and said I've been late enough times to get suspended."

"Then you better get here early from now on. Don't mess around with him anymore, Corey. Just do what he says," Emily said.

"It's not like I do it on purpose."

"I have never been late," Emily added as an after-thought.

"Thanks Emily," I replied sarcastically.

"What did your mother want last night?" she asked, changing the subject to an earnest one.

"Ahhh, not much. I don't know why she called your house looking for me. It was nothing," I said, but couldn't look at Emily when I lied.

"That's strange, Corey. She sounded really upset on the phone. That's not like her. She's always so strong about things. You can never tell if something is bothering her, but I could tell last night."

"Maybe so," I said, hoping this conversation would end quickly. I couldn't tell Emily the real news, for one simple reason. I had no intentions of doing anything differently. I would continue to bide my time until graduation, leave, and never come back. Emily would never understand that. She would despise me if she knew my mother was sick and asking for my help, and I wasn't giving it.

Chapter 14

MY ROUTINE did not change after the walk that night.
I did not have the answers to my mother's problems, and
I wondered why she even took the time to tell me. What
could I do to make it better? I decided to steer clear of
Linda Wails, just like I always had. She can work it out on
her own, I thought. After all, she was the strongest person
I had ever known.

A week later I went home after practice. My mother
was sitting at the kitchen bar when I walked in the door.

"Your father tells me next week is the first game of the
playoffs," she said, handing me a plate of home cooked
food.

"Yes Ma'am," I answered, eyeing the plate, wondering
if I should eat the pork chops or the mashed potatoes first.
My mother looked thinner than normal, but not sick. She
was always trying to lose weight anyway, so I figured it was
a good thing. She was probably trying to be healthy now
that she has cancer again. I had seen it all before.

"I washed your uniform and hung it up in the closet," she said.

Now I know she is sick, I thought in jest. She never spent an ounce of energy on anything that had to do with baseball.

I ate my dinner, thanked her for making it, and for washing my uniform. She was standing over the sink cleaning the dishes when I said good night.

"Can I have a hug?" my mother asked, taking off the dish gloves and putting her arms out. I stood like a statue, making no movement towards her. She came to me instead.

"You'll be as tall as your father some day," my mother said. The tone of her voice and the look in her eyes was just like the night of our walk, when she was seeing and thinking too many things at once; the present, the past, and the future mingling together in one long, infinitely complex web; memories of days gone and moments of the here and now where every second seems like eternity.

She put her arms around me and pulled me close to her. I felt her chin on my forehead, and could feel her thinking. She pushed me away, just enough to look at me.

"And just as handsome," she said.

After another strange second, she said, "Have you thought about what we talked about the other night—about you and I working this out together?"

"No, I've been busy with baseball practice," I answered.

I saw her disappointment. Her eyes went blank, her smile was replaced with tight lips, and her eyes began to water.

"All right," she said in a weak voice, released me, and

turned back to the sink to finish the dishes.

For some reason I stood there. I remained in the kitchen staring at my mother. I noticed her blouse quivering against her back. She was holding it all in; her emotions were welling up inside of her like an earthquake, trembling on the surface.

I wanted to go to her, throw my arms around her neck, give her a kiss, and tell her that I loved her, but I had no idea how. I could not remember the last time I had done any of those things. It seemed like the thing to do, and yet I couldn't do it, so I walked away. I was almost across the living room when she called my name.

"Yes Ma'am?" I replied.

"I'm coming to your next game," she said, proud of the idea.

She hadn't been to one of my baseball games in years. I wondered if she knew I was a pitcher.

"Sounds good," I said, and continued across the living room. I stopped just at the French doors leading to the hall, just like I had done a week earlier, on the night she told me she had cancer; the night she told me she was going to die. I had the same view tonight as I had then.

Her shoulders, always pulled back and always strong, were crumbling. She was supporting herself on the counter with her right hand; her left was moving beneath the counter. She turned quickly and headed into the hallway leading to the pantry. Her walk was fast and slanted. She was limping and clutching at her side. She turned sharply into the bathroom without switching on the light. I heard the toilet seat come up and the sounds of her vomiting uncontrollably. I heard her gasps in between each spell.

After several minutes, she said, "Oh God" before another series of spasms. I heard her crying, mumbling inaudible words, and gasping for air in between each wave. Standing in the doorway, halfway across the house listening as if I were a neighbor who didn't want to get involved, I wished I had kissed my mother good night. Where is my dad? I thought. Doesn't he know how sick she is? He should be taking care of her.

I heard her get to her feet and turn on the water faucet. I heard her talking to herself. "You can do it Linda," she said. I heard a loud sniffle as she cleared her throat, and I guessed she was straightening her hair and checking herself in the mirror. I felt a sharp pain in my chest. The next time I feel something I am going to act on it, I told myself. Regret is a hard pill to swallow.

When I heard the water stop running in the sink, I slipped away down the hall. I knew she would not want me to see her in such a way, and I didn't want her to know I had been listening.

Chapter 15

"**W**AILS, THAT'S ENOUGH SON," Cavanaugh yelled.

I had been throwing for an hour solid, and Mike had a grimace on his face because of the bruise I was leaving on his hand. The harder I threw, the better I felt. My arm did not seem like it was attached to my body. I could throw for hours and not even feel it.

"Just a few more, Mike," I called down to my catcher as he was standing up.

"I'm not in the habit of repeating myself, Wails," Cavanaugh yelled. "Since you've got so much energy— everybody grab a bat. We're gonna take some live batting practice."

The team was ecstatic about the event. Each man headed to the bat bag, grabbed a stick, and formed a line.

Manny was first. He stepped up to the plate, tucked his gold chain under his jersey and shot me a wide grin. I threw the first one right by him.

"Oooo-Weee, Wails. You're bringin' it tonight," he said,

and stepped out of the box.

He choked up on the bat and got down to business. He laid down a perfect bunt, rapped a line drive over second base, and sent a shot up the middle.

"Is that all you got?" Manny said, and tapped home plate.

"That's enough, Manny. Fitz, you're up," Cavanaugh yelled.

Fitz took his stance, rapped on the plate, and waited. When I heard the loud thump of the aluminum bat, I knew the ball was going out of the park. I turned and watched it land just outside the fence in dead center.

"I gave you that one, Fitz. Just to make you feel good," I said.

"By all means, don't hold back Wails," Cavanaugh chided.

After the first nine hitters, I thought my arm was going to fall off. I thought darkness would be my saving grace, but when Cavanaugh turned on the field lights, I knew we were going to be at it a while.

I pitched to every player on the team. Well into the night we took live batting practice until I could hardly throw another pitch. Even Duffers got base hits. I thought my arm would fall from my shoulder, but there was no reprieve from Cavanaugh. After Stoney sent four out of five fastballs over the fence, Cavanaugh called us into the dugout.

"It's a dern good thing you don't have to pitch against us, Wails. We would eat you alive," Cavanaugh said. "I want you all to take a seat."

"Are there any balls left coach, or did we break 'em all?" Manny asked to everyone's amusement.

We were all seated in the dugout and Cavanaugh stood in front of us; a hand on his knee, one foot in the dugout, and the other on the field.

"Gentlemen, the playoffs start next week. From here on out every game could be the last one. I want you to remember that when you tighten the laces on your cleats, and you get ready to step onto this field.

"I have coached most of you since you were knee high to a grasshopper. I have watched you grow up and become fine athletes, and I am proud of every one of you, not because of how you play, how fast you can run, or how well you hit the ball, but because of your dedication to this game and to this team.

"We have spent years practicing for just a few hours of game time. You have all taken a thousand practice swings for every at bat in a game. You have all fielded a thousand balls for every one that has come your way when it matters. And what does that tell you—we aren't here for just the games. They're only a measure of our dedication. I want you boys to remember that."

After Cavanaugh's talk I walked back to the locker room with the team. It was the first time in weeks that I didn't stay after to take extra cuts.

As we were crossing the field, I noticed my father standing beside his car in the parking lot. Cole saw him at the same time as me.

"Hey Mr. Wails," Cole called out and waved.

"You boys looked good out there tonight. I'm counting on you to go all the way," my father said. "Corey, come here son, I want to speak to you."

I told the guys I would catch up with them in the locker

room and wandered out to the parking lot. I didn't take a straight line, but meandered, wondering what my father had to say to me. It wasn't like him to intervene.

"How's your arm?" he asked, as I reached the car.

"It's fine," I replied.

"Have you been icing it at night? You know how important it is."

"Yes sir. I'm taking care of it," I said. "But I don't suppose you're here to talk about my arm."

"No, I'm not. You know why I'm here," he said evenly; his face stern.

"I've a pretty good idea," I answered.

"I am doing all I can for your mother, but it's not me she needs right now. You're disappointing me son," my father said. "I have always taken up for you—always. Every time your mother tells me how selfish you are, how thoughtless and uncaring her son has become, I take up for you. But now I'm not sure if she isn't right. Your behavior is inexcusable. I can't make you do the right thing—no one can. It's up to you and no one else. Frankly, I am beginning to wonder."

"Wonder about what?" I replied, put off by his accusations.

"If you care about anything," he stated harshly.

I had no reply to that. I respected my father; I looked up to him, and I admired him. That admiration came crashing down around me as his words cut into me.

I held my tongue. Who was he to judge? Where was he when the fighting was going on? Whose side did he always take? He had no right to judge me.

"Do you have nothing to say for yourself? Nothing to

make me think differently?" he asked.

I knew he was searching. He was trying to get inside my thoughts for the first time. He had waited until the direst of circumstances to try to learn what made his son tick.

"That woman is no mother of mine," I replied. "She died a long time ago."

With that I turned and started walking away. A lot of firsts were occurring in my life, so it didn't surprise me when I didn't feel scared for speaking my mind unadulterated to my father.

My words floored him. He stood in utter disbelief of what I had just said.

"What happened to you, Corey? For all the world, I can't see it," he replied in a weak tone. "Your mother loves you. If you would give her a chance you would see it."

I heard him. I heard him loud and clear. I heard my father, Robert Wails, say the word love. It was probably the first time in my life I had ever heard it come from his lips.

"It's my fault—it's always my fault," I yelled. "Well, I'll tell you what, if I'm not around then she can find someone else to blame," I said, and continued walking. The more distance I put between us, the more enraged he became.

"You're incapable. Do you hear me! You are incapable of love," he yelled.

I turned quickly. My father and I stood thirty yards a part and he was shouting at me about love.

"Do you love me, Dad?" I asked point blank.

"Of course I do. Haven't you always known that?"

"I know you do everything you can for your family— whatever it takes to make us happy, whatever you have to sacrifice for us, but have you ever told me that you love me?" I asked.

"What are you talking about?" he replied, his voice trailing off.

"Am I supposed to know what love is because you buy me a new glove, you buy me a new bat, you take me to practice every day since I was five, you coach me, you push me, and teach me how to play baseball. It's this game that I love. Am I to be blamed? Am I to all of a sudden change what I have become? I've spent my whole life working on what you see in front of you. Are you going to change what you have become and what that woman in our house has become? Do you expect me to throw my arms around her and tell her I love her? After everything we've been through. Huh? Do you?" I said defiantly.

"Yes I do," he replied evenly.

"Then why can't you do the same with me? Why are we still standing thirty yards apart? Huh Dad? Why?" I yelled. "I'll tell you why, because the love you are talking about died a long time ago. And you know it."

When I walked away from my father that night, I knew irreparable damage had been done. My father had never said such things to me, nor me to him. He hardly ever said a word about anything that had to do with emotions. I always thought the giant was emotionless, but there he stood crying out loud about something called love.

Chapter 16

I AWOKE STARTLED. I had been having a nightmare. The horizon was bleak. Dark clouds were gathering. The wind picked up, lightning bolts were streaking to the ground, and thunder like cannon blasts was rolling through the hills.

The herd of cattle the old man and I were tending had become uneasy in the approaching storm. They had congregated under a lone oak tree that stood in the middle of a fallow field.

"Come a lightning bolt, and we're liable to lose the whole herd," the old man said. "Get on out of here, Get!" My grandfather was yelling and slapping at the cattle's hides with a glove. "Get a move on!"

Cattle were coming and going; uneasy as they were, their hooves churned the earth into a cloud of dust. The old man was knocked off his feet. The cattle's heads were rising and falling with their heavy shoulders, as their hooves came crashing down, over and over. The sky became dark and laden down. I was running towards the old man, wondering why I hadn't left sooner, wishing I could run faster, screaming at an ignorant herd of livestock.

The nightmare lingered, but consciously I heard my father's voice, "It'll be OK, Linda. It's almost over." The shower was running and my mother was half screaming and half crying. In a gargled voice she was calling my father's name.

I jumped out of bed and rushed to the bathroom. My father was supporting my mother's weight at her waist; her head was hanging lifeless from her shoulders and vomit was pouring from her mouth. I noticed there was blood on the tile floor and on the carpet.

"Get some towels, son," my father said as soon as he saw me.

"It'll be over soon, honey. Hang in there," he said soothingly to my mother.

I was confused. How long has this been going on? I wondered. Have I become so good at avoidance that I could miss this?

I came back with the towels, placed them on the counter, and peered into the bathroom. My mother's body was limp; her legs were stretched out behind her, locked at the knees, and my father was still supporting all of her weight.

"Your mother fell in the shower and hit her head. Call 911 and get an ambulance here!" my father said quickly.

"Noooo," my mother yelled.

I stood in the doorway staring at her in disbelief. I was so used to taking her orders I was still obeying them. I did not move. Three quick gasps of air and she regained control of her breathing. She bent her knees so they touched the floor, and the strain lessened on my fathers' arms. She placed a hand on the edge of the tub, supporting some of her own weight. A few more deep breaths; she slouched down to the floor, and turned around. My father grabbed a towel, unfolded it, and wrapped it around her head. I could see more clearly now that he had moved, and noticed a cut above her right eye.

"Corey, go get some ice," he said.

I was half way down the hall before all of his words had escaped.

"Linda, are you sure you don't want to go to the hospital?" he was asking her when I returned.

She was slumped down, back against the tub, breathing like I did after twenty of Cavanaugh's suicides. One leg was bent, and the other was stretched across the floor. She took a few deep breaths before answering my father.

"No, Robert. I don't want to go to the hospital," she replied defiantly, having regained enough strength to be her normal self. "How bad is the cut on my head?" she asked.

"I don't think you need stitches, but it's going be a knot," my father answered.

As my mother pushed the towel back and raised her chin, she saw me for the first time. No words were spoken, and yet so much was exchanged between our eyes.

It was her eyes that were dry and crystal clear, and mine that were wet and hazy. The towel my father had placed over the cut covered her hair and most of her head; and with no makeup to disrupt the strong lines of her face, her angled cheek bones and large, brown eyes were prominent. No matter how ugly her disposition could be, my mother could never hide her physical beauty—not even now.

As strange as it seemed, she had a look of victory in her eyes. Her look was puzzling to me. What emotion could create this silent strength; this look of having accomplished something extraordinary; the slight crease of her lips that looked like the beginning of a smile?

Her shoulders relaxed, dropping down into their resting position, and her breathing returned to normal. The sickness was over. It had come and gone like a violent summer shower.

Our eyes were still locked when she reached a hand out. Instinctively, I grabbed her wrist. With her fingertips resting in the palm of my hand, I felt the tremor in her muscles. I suddenly realized why she had been acting so strangely; why she had bothered to tell me about her sickness; why she was seeing, thinking, and feeling so much in every moment. Her eyes told me what her courage lacked the ability to put into words: "You see son, I am dying, and it's not going to be ten years from now. I need your help and you need mine."

There was a battle going on inside me. Part of me wanted to help this woman, and part of me wanted nothing to do with it. I do not need any help from her I told myself, and she does not deserve any from me. Looking at her lying there in a pile, back against the tub, bleeding, and breathing heavy from the nausea, I felt sorry for her. I felt pity for her. I thought about that terrible emotion —pity. To pity Linda Wails was worse than to despise her and leave her alone. If she knew what I was thinking she would not want any help from me.

I gently let go of her hand, rested it in her lap, and turned towards my father. "Do you need anything else Dad?"

He made no reply, only looked at my mother with a long face of helplessness.

Her eyes were begging me and I walked away. I turned my back on her just like she had always done to me, and it created the worst emotion I have ever felt. I was as unworthy of being her son as she was of being my mother. An eye for an eye I told myself, but believed it with only half my heart; the other half wanted to hug the stranger lying on the bathroom floor and tell her that I loved her, because she was my mother; the only one I would ever have.

I walked out of the bathroom without saying another word and got ready for school. My father can take care of her, I told myself. It's not my responsibility.

As I was backing out of the driveway, my father came through the back door. He was waving his arms for me to stop, so I did. He walked quickly towards my jeep.

"Son," my father said solemnly, and said no more. To be certain, the Wails were each carrying one third of the weight of the world on their shoulders. My mother had dropped her burden, my father's was sliding off his back, while I alone heaved to and pushed onward.

I saw his indecision; I guessed what he had come to say, but heard only, "I may be late to the game. I need to stay here until Mrs. Jenkins comes to watch your mother."

"Yes sir," I replied.

He turned and walked back to the house.

There had been a late season frost the night before; I noticed ice crystals on the blades of grass. On the porch balcony were two flower boxes of chrysanthemums. My mother had draped a quilt over each box to protect her flowers from the freezing night. Something about the scene struck me as odd; the forethought that went into placing quilts so delicately over flowers, and so timely as to preserve their life seemed like a strange thing for my mother to worry about now. The scene lingered in my mind, as the nightmare had earlier.

It was a cold ride without the top on my jeep. The air was damp with half frozen moisture. Shards of ice were pelting my face, my warm blood was rising to the surface of my cold skin, making the hair stand up all over my body. I was shivering and yet I felt nothing. I had no thoughts, I had no feelings, only emptiness did I feel that morning, like there was a gaping hole inside of me that nothing could ever fill.

Twice I let the same person win the battle over what to do about my mother. Should I help her? Do I need her help? I asked myself those questions, and wondered what I had to gain from helping her. It is too late. Nothing can make things better between us now.

All of a sudden, I realized the time. I looked at the clock on the dashboard. It was 8:15. I smashed the gas pedal to the floor and raced down the street. I grew colder and colder as the wind passed over my skin faster and harder. If Mr. Torant sees me I am through. I was doing 60 miles an hour on a side street, when the urgency that had risen so quickly passed.

Slowly, without my foot applying pressure to the gas pedal, my jeep came to a rolling stop. Who am I? I asked myself for perhaps the first time in my life. Is this the person I want to be, or is this the person I have become?

I sat there for a long while, trying to make sense of something in my life.

When I regained myself, I continued to school, mechanically and with little thought. When I pulled into
the parking lot, there was Mr. Torant. He was practically
waiting on me.

I looked at myself in the rearview mirror, checking to
see if he would know I had been crying. It was a sign of
weakness, and not one that I wanted him to see.

"I didn't think you could do it," Mr. Torant said, walking
up to my jeep. "You lasted less than a week."

I made no reply in my defense.

"Well, Mr. Corey. You've played your last baseball
game at Hillcrest. Keep this up, and you'll be lucky if you
graduate," Mr. Torant said. "I'll notify Coach Cavanaugh
of my decision to take you off the team."

Any other day in my life that news would not only have
crushed me, it would have brought such tears to my eyes
that rivers would run deep, but not today. His words had
no impact.

"Did you hear me, Corey? I said you're off the team,"
he continued, searching for some response. There was
none to be had.

"I heard you, Mr. Torant," I said indifferently. All
around me were nothing but clouds, so dark and so thick,
no light shone through at all.

"Don't think I won't keep my end of our bargain. I will."

Mr. Torant's words filled nothing but a void in the sky.
For the first time in my life, I realized there may be something more important than my own dreams.

Chapter 17

I WENT THROUGH THE MOTIONS of school that day, head down, eyes staring at the ground. I couldn't get the sight of my mother's sickness out of my head for the life of me. I talked very little, saying only what I had to and nothing more. I purposefully stayed out of the path of Emily, Cole, Seth, Mike, all of them; I couldn't stand to face a soul. I snuck around school like I had snuck around my house for years. When the last class of the day rolled around, I knew there was no escaping Emily.

I took my seat next to her and she immediately started asking questions.

"Where have you been all day, Corey? No one has seen you," she said inquisitively.

"I've been here all day," I said. "I don't know."

"You don't know what?"

"Where I've been I guess," I answered.

"Corey," what is wrong with you?" Emily asked in a concerned tone.

I had my hands over my face and was staring down at the desk top. Emily put her face between my arms and looked up at me. There was no way to avert my eyes from hers.

"Tell me what's the matter?" she asked again.

I knew I had to tell her. I had to tell her everything, only I had waited so long that now I didn't know how.

"Is it your mother again?" she asked. "Cole said you didn't come to Mr. Stewart's class today. Were you late again?"

"It's everything, Emily. Yes, I was late again, and …."

"Did Mr. Torant kick you off the team!" she exclaimed.

"Yes." I answered flatly.

Emily turned so sharply that her desk moved with her body. "Corey, what are you going to do? You have scholarships riding on baseball. He can't just do that. He can't ruin your life …"

"Yes he can. He already did it."

"Corey," Emily said in a long sigh. "What about the team? What did Seth and Cole say? What about ..."

"They don't know yet," I replied, cutting Emily off. "Baseball isn't even what's bothering me. Not now."

When I said that, Emily knew it was something really big; for me not to care about getting kicked off the baseball team it had to be of monumental importance.

"Corey, you're scaring me," Emily said and leaned in closer to me. "What else? What else could there be? Is Mr. Torant going to expel you? He definitely can't do that."

"It's my mother, Emily. She has cancer again. Worse this time," I replied.

"No … when. How long have you …"

"She told me the night she called your house—three

weeks ago," I replied.

Emily said nothing. She let my words and all of my actions sink in.

"Corey, I don't understand you," Emily said. "Why didn't you tell me when I asked? And why haven't you told me until now?"

"I don't know. I just couldn't."

"You couldn't tell me that your mother has cancer? How is she? Oh, I guess you wouldn't know. How many times have you seen her since she told you," Emily said, her tone turning harsh. "Once, twice maybe?"

"Twice," I said to my own embarrassment.

"You're awful Corey Wails. Awful," Emily said, and began collecting her books.

Suddenly, as if the other questions were now of no importance, she said, "How bad is it?"

That was the question I didn't want to answer, but I knew I had to tell Emily the truth.

"She says she is going to die," I replied.

Emily gasped in horror. Her eyes cut through me like I was the most evil person in the world. She snatched up her books and went running out of the room. On the way out the door, the teacher called her name.

Emily turned sharply. "I'm sorry, Mrs. Engels, but something has come up. I have to leave," Emily said with tears streaming down her cheeks.

I remained seated at my desk for the duration of the class. I didn't hear one single word spoken by the teacher. I heard only the ringing in my ears of Emily Vallent telling me that I was awful, my father telling me that I was incapable, and my mother telling me that I was a selfish little brat. It was in that hour that I felt something inside of me yearning to get out.

When the last buzzer sounded, I headed straight to the locker room to speak with Cavanaugh. I found him in his coach's office, seated behind his desk, looking over the line-up for tonight's game. He glanced up at me when I came into his office, and went back to the papers in front of him.

"Coach, I need to talk to you," I said.

"I already know Wails. Torant spoke to me this morning. There's nothing I can do for you, son," Cavanaugh said evenly.

I noticed smudges on the paper where he had erased a name from the number nine spot on the batting list; Roly was now written where my name had been. I sat staring at the roster in disbelief that this day, the entire affair, was even happening to me. It just didn't seem real. After several minutes of dead silence, Cavanaugh dropped his pencil and looked up at me. His eyes were harsh.

"In case I have lead you to believe all these years that baseball is the means by which we reach our end, I apologize. Baseball is a discipline, son. What happens on the field is no different than what happens off. What do you do when you walk a hitter?"

"I bear down on the next one," I replied from rote memory.

"What do you do when you're ahead in the count?"

"I waste a pitch," I answered.

"What does the team do when they're down runs," he said.

"We pull together."

"What does the team do when they lose a player?"

"We pick up the slack."

"That's what we'll have to do now. Make no mistake about who you have let down today. It's not me and it's not yourself, it's your teammates. They were counting on you to pitch for this ball club.

"I don't care if a player is the best in the county or the worst in the state, I only ask that they give 110%. That doesn't mean just at game time. By being a member of this ball club your responsibility is not only for yourself but for this team. How many times have I told you that? It extends into every part of your life; coming to school on time is no exception."

"Yes sir," I replied.

"The team is going to miss you sorely," Cavanaugh said. He stood up from his desk and placed his hand on my head. I felt against my skull the huge ring he wore for having been a pitcher for a team that won the World Series.

"You'll learn something from this," he said. "I will be gravely disappointed in you if you don't."

In that sad manner, Cavanaugh left me sitting in his office, while he went to the locker room to ready his players for the first game of the playoffs.

Chapter 18

AFTER MEETING WITH CAVANAUGH, I didn't know where to go or what to do. Baseball was all I knew. I couldn't stand to see Cole or Seth and have to explain to them that I had been kicked off the team. I thought about going to Torant and telling him about my mother, and that was why I was late. For a moment, I thought there may be a way out of this yet. I wondered if I got back on the team if Cavanaugh would put me back in the line-up. I doubted it. I wondered if Torant would revoke his decision if I told him my mother had cancer. I wanted to use that excuse, but knew I had no right. My soul was aching for the right thing to do, but for the life of me I couldn't figure out what it was.

Where did Emily go? I wondered. I guessed she was at my house with my mother. What will my dad say when he finds out I have been kicked off the team? That thought made my palms sweat. Something as simple as getting somewhere on time was going to stand in the way of my future. I wondered if Littleman would still make me an offer if I didn't finish the season? I wondered if the college scouts that had seen me in the other games would still be interested if I missed the playoffs? I wondered if Torant would sabotage me further with poor recommendations?

"Wails, where are you headed?"

I knew that voice belonged to Todd Manny, our star center fielder. I looked up and saw him leaning nonchalantly on the side of his car with a pretty young girl in his arms. He was wearing his baseball jersey with the front open. The girl's hand was on his chest muscles, and fingering his gold chain. Manny was grinning, like he always was.

"I'm off the team, Todd. Torant kicked me off this morning."

Manny put a hand on the girl's shoulder, moving her aside, and he walked over to me. The smile left his face.

"What are you talking about Wails? He can't do that—not with the playoffs just starting."

"Well, he did. I just talked to Cavanaugh about it."

"What did Coach say?"

"He said there was nothing he could do about it. Torant told him this morning that I was kicked off the team. Cavanaugh can't do a thing about it."

Manny looked around for a second, like there was something else that could be done. He looked back at the school, and then at me.

"Wails, I've never played a baseball game without you."

"Believe me, I know that better than you. I've had all day to think about it," I answered.

"Why did Torant kick you off the team?"

"For being late 16 times this year."

"Damn Wails. Can't you get to school on time?"

I made no reply.

"I don't know who's gonna do the pitching now. You've really messed us up haven't you?" Manny said.

"I didn't mean to, Manny. I'd give anything to be out there tonight. It's all we've talked about since we were kids."

"And now look at you … you're not even gonna be there," Manny said. "Sixteen times, Wails? Did he warn you?"

"He warned me last week," I replied, feeling the full weight of my own actions. "Good luck tonight, Todd," I said, and headed to my jeep.

Just as I got in the driver's seat, Manny yelled out to me.

"You did as much as anyone to get us here. I'll try to remind the team."

I left the school and drove around for a while, undecided on where to go or what to do. No more baseball, I thought. What does that mean? Cavanaugh said I would learn something from this, and I wondered what it would be. Maybe this is fate, I thought. Maybe this is what I get for making a game my life.

As I was driving and thinking, I found myself headed to Emily's house. I drove by and didn't see her car in the driveway, and I guessed she was at my house. Reluctantly, I started home.

When I reached my house, Emily's car wasn't there either, and I wondered where she could have gone. I parked, and walked inside. My mother was sitting on the couch in the living room.

"What are you doing here, Corey?" she asked in a very calm, pleasant voice.

Her comment struck a chord. 'What are you doing here,' she had said. I was standing in my own house being asked by my mother, 'what are you doing here?' I was never here, I thought.

"I forgot my socks for the game," I lied.

I noticed the cut above her eye and a bruise that was forming around her eye. I thought about asking her how she was, but didn't. I didn't want to bring up anything as a reminder of the morning's events.

"Emily stopped by to see me," my mother said. "She's such a sweet girl."

"Yes Ma'am."

"Did you tell her that I was sick again?" my mother asked very casually.

"Yes. I told her," I said, puzzled by my mother's lackadaisical attitude.

"Did she not mention that?" I asked, wondering what words had been exchanged.

"No. She said she just came by to say hello, because she hadn't seen me in a while."

"Are you still coming to my game tonight?" I asked.

"Of course," she replied, as if she had never missed one.

I went to my room and got a pair of white socks, so my mother would not know the real reason I had come home was to check on her.

Chapter 19

I DROVE TOWARD THE SCHOOL, only instead of going all the way there I took a side street that ran behind the baseball field. I parked on a corner and trudged through the woods for some distance, before reaching the chain link fence that ran around the outfield.

The team was warming up their arms and legs, playing catch, and swinging bats. I heard very little chatter and saw no mouths moving. I found a spot in between two wooden advertisement banners and stretched out on the ground to watch the game.

I had never seen the field from this perspective, from the outside looking in. The field looked different; it looked bigger, and empty. I scanned the crowd and noticed the Vallent's all sitting together: Emily, her mother, and her father. Mr. Vallent was speaking, but I could tell Emily wasn't listening to whatever he was saying. She was sitting idle, staring off. I saw my father standing along the fence near the bull pen. He was looking around, almost in a panic, inspecting every player. I knew exactly what he was thinking: Where is Corey? Where the hell is Corey?

Our team and theirs, the Moore's Creek Panthers, lined up down the base paths and the Star Spangled Banner was sung by the school choir. Maybe it was because I was watching through a fence that the affair seemed to lack energy.

The field cleared. Both teams went into their dugouts. Cavanaugh said a few words from the steps, and went to his post at first base. A moment later, Moore's Creek took the field for inning one of game one of the state playoffs.

While the pitcher was warming up, I noticed my mother walking towards the bleachers. She was looking around at all the familiar faces, ones she had not seen in a long time. I noticed a lot of waves being exchanged and pleasant smiles. She found a seat on the third row of the bleachers closest to our dugout and sat down. She was smiling and relaxed, not scanning the park looking for me like my father was.

A moment later my father took a seat next to her. He rocked forward, put his elbows on his knees and took a long, deep breath. My mother leaned in and kissed him on the cheek. He didn't as much as turn his head.

The Moore's Creek pitcher really proved himself in the first inning. He covered a Todd Manny bunt perfectly and threw out our speed demon at first. I had seen only one other pitcher capable of that kind of agility. Next he retired Fitz and then Miller. The top of the inning was over in a hurry.

The Bulldogs didn't come rushing out of the dugout like they were hungry for their defense, but sauntered to their positions. Cavanaugh laid into them.

"Pick up the slack, gentleman," he called out in a harsh tone.

I was so anxious and torn apart when the umpire tossed the game ball to Roly, that I wanted to climb the fence and go running onto the field, shouting something; only I had no idea what it would be. I found my father in the stands and noticed the frustrated look on his face.

Roly finished his warm-ups and the infielders headed to the mound, like we always did before the first pitch was thrown. My father got up from his seat and walked briskly to the dugout. He stuck his head around the corner and said something to Cavanaugh. My coach returned some words, leaned his head out of the dugout and spit. I knew exactly what had been exchanged.

As my father returned to the bleachers, I could tell by his gait that he was livid. He walked quickly and machine-like. He took his seat next my mother. She put her hand on his knee and whispered something to him. His expression didn't change. His jaw was set tight. He clapped his hands together hard and yelled, "Come on boys."

The bottom of the first inning didn't go so well for us. Roly's first opponent proved better than he, sending a solid line drive over Fitz's head at short. The batter stood on second base, and every player in the Moore's Creek dugout was on their feet. The next batter dropped a lazy grounder down the third base line. As it dribbled down the line, Stoney decided not to play it. He watched it, and watched it, hoping it would hit a pebble or a rut in the field and turn foul. The ball passed the bag, still in play, and the umpire threw up his hands and yelled, "Fair ball."

Cavanaugh jumped to his feet and yelled, "You gotta

play that ball, Stoney! ... Come on now, use your head."

With runners on first and second and no outs in the first, Roly was already in trouble. On the next pitch, everyone was moving. The batter made solid contact and sent a shell up the middle, almost knocking Roly off the mound. When the smoke cleared, it was 1 to 0, no outs and runners on second and third. The pace continued. Miller bobbled a grounder, allowing an unearned run to score. Parker missed a cutoff throw and a single turned to a double. Moore's Creek capitalized on every little mistake.

Cavanaugh was pacing back and forth, back and forth. He was tossing a baseball in his hand. I could hear it popping in his palm, even from where I sat outside the fence. He came out of the dugout and stood on the first baseline. He eyed the team, but said nothing. Roly shrugged his shoulders, like he didn't know what to do. He was pitching a good game, but getting no support in the field.

"This is a team. Now play like one," Cavanaugh said sternly, and returned to the dugout.

His words had little effect. The Bulldogs didn't pull together, and Moore's Creek rallied for four runs in the first inning. It was the laziest display of baseball I had ever seen.

The affair did not change. The second, third, fourth, and fifth innings were all the same, only Cavanaugh stopped wasting his words on deaf ears.

Inning after inning, while the team botched plays in the field and swung half heartedly at the plate, Cavanaugh sat in the dugout chomping on his tobacco in silent resignation.

Moore's Creek put more runs on the board in the sixth, bringing the score to 9-0. Roly had to earn his keep by strik-

ing out the last two batters in the sixth inning, but there was
no excitement to be found in the aces. He walked off the
mound, head hung low. It was the same with everyone; they
all walked off the field like soldiers from a lost battle.

Chapter 20

CAVANAUGH WAS SILENT for five innings, but watching his players walk off the diamond was the last straw. He shot out of the dugout. His voice boomed across the field.

"You men will not walk around on my baseball field. I want to see some damn hustle!" he yelled. "Win or lose, it makes no difference, but you're not going to do either one walking, not on my field."

Everyone's pace quickened in an instant. Cavanaugh sent every man into the dugout, one and all, while he himself stood on the lip of the field. He paced back and forth in front of his team. His mouth was moving, but I couldn't hear what he was saying. I had a pretty good idea though. The team was staring down at the ground, but all of a sudden their heads snapped to attention. Cavanaugh singled out Miller and then Parker; he pointed to the field; he motioned to the mound and then the plate. He reached in and grabbed Cole by the jersey and led him to the on-deck circle. Cavanaugh rubbed his hands together and said something to him. Cole nodded and started towards the plate. Cavanaugh, in unlike fashion, jogged down the third base line.

Ray Cavanaugh had coached every one of us for years. He had followed this team from Babe Ruth league, to junior high, to high school. In all those years I had never seen him take any post other than first base, but he now stood at third base, arms folded over his chest, watching the action from a seemingly distant perspective. From this new post, he would command his team on the base paths.

Cole drove the first pitch to shallow left field. It was an easy single, and not much more. But Cavanaugh was waving him on.

"Stretch it out, stretch it out," Cavanaugh yelled.

As Cole neared second base, the ball was already in the air.

"Hit the dirt," Cavanaugh called out.

Cole went into the bag head first beating the tag by inches.

"Now that's hustle," Cavanaugh yelled.

Cole wiped his pants and took his lead. Parker stepped up to the plate. Cavanaugh brushed a few signals off his sleeves, and Parker readied his bat. He got all of a fastball and sent it to center field. The Moore's Creek outfielder played the ball quickly, only he didn't expect Cole to try to score all the way from second base on a single. The Moore's Creek center fielder lazily removed the ball from his glove, like a player whose team is up nine runs. Cavanaugh was waving Cole on. The Moore's Creek coach stepped out of the dugout shouting:

"Hit your cut-off man, there's gonna be a play at the

plate."

It was too late. The center fielder tried to recover, but Cole was more than half way home. When Cole crossed the plate, the Moore's Creek coach took his hat off and wrung it out in his hands. "Look sharp out there," he yelled.

"Come on now Posie. Keep it going son," Cavanaugh said.

Mike Posie straightened his helmet, rubbed his hands together, gripped his bat, and stepped into the box. Cavanaugh signaled for a hit and run. I perked up in anticipation of the play.

Posie swung hard. Parker was moving. The ball went foul, giving away the hit and run. The Moore's Creek infielders crept in towards the plate. Cavanaugh cleared the signals, giving our catcher full reign. He sent the next pitch to right field. The ball bounced off the fence not more than ten feet from where I was hiding behind the sign.

The fielder played the ball perfectly. He turned and fired it back to the infield. To my disbelief Cavanaugh was waving Parker through third base, sending him towards home plate.

"Move, move, move ..." Cavanaugh was yelling. His arms were moving like a windmill. Parker was digging, and every player in the dugout was on their feet cheering him on.

The throw came late; Parker scored, and Posie took an extra base because of the play at the plate. He stood on second.

The crowd went wild; lights were flashing, the local television crews angled their cameras from the Moore's

Creek dugout to ours. The Moore's Creek coach made a visit to the mound, rightfully so, three back to back doubles warranted a visit.

Next up was Jackson, then Roly, then Godfrey. Singles were had all the way around. Next was Stoney. The pitcher bore down on him, giving him two inside fast balls that Stoney could do nothing with. With an 0 and 2 count our lefty power house laid down a bunt. It took everyone in the park by surprise. The pitcher was slow coming off the mound and the second baseman didn't cover first. Stoney beat the throw and Roly advanced to third.

"That's using your head, Stoney," Cavanaugh yelled.

Stoney stood on first base grinning. Cavanaugh rapped on Roly's helmet and said something that made him grin.

The crowd got to their feet in applause. The Hillcrest Bulldog's notorious homerun hitter had just laid down a bunt for a base hit. For a second I forgot that I was hiding and almost shouted out my own applause.

Timmy Duffers stepped out of the dugout holding the score book in his hands. "Top of the line-up," he called, and read out the order, just because we always did. "Manny, Fitz, Miller!" There was energy in his voice.

Manny singled, Fitz singled, Manny stole third, and Miller drove them in with a double. Man, they went through the whole line-up. The tables turned and the Hillcrest Bulldogs were right back on top of things.

Moore's Creek brought in a new pitcher, but it didn't help their cause. Cavanaugh was pushing everyone on the base paths and Moore's Creek couldn't keep up. We stretched singles to doubles, we stole bases, we squeezed out runs, and by the end of the inning we had taken the lead: 10-9.

It was the most exciting inning of baseball I had ever been a part of. I was right there with them; not even the distance or the fence stood in the way.

Roly didn't come back to the mound in the eighth; instead Cavanaugh sent in our reliever, Timmy Duffers. I knew what Cavanaugh was thinking. With me gone, he would have to stretch just two pitchers as far as he could. The momentum had changed, so he was saving Roly's arm for the next start; a start that should have been mine.

While Duffers was warming up, I scanned the bleachers. I was looking for Littleman and the other scouts that I knew were there. I saw all the scouts seated together. They were all wearing wide smiles and talking jovially. I wondered what, and about whom, they were speaking. The game had been a team effort through and through. No one had taken the lime light, unless of course they were recruiting coaches.

When my eyes reached the far end of the bleachers where my mother had been seated, I noticed she was standing up talking with Mr. Torant. My father was still seated on the edge of the bleachers. He was watching our new pitcher intently, but had his head cocked to hear what Mr. Torant and my mother were saying.

My mother put her hand on the cut above her eye, and made some movements with her arms. Mr. Torant was nodding his head, and listening to her. After a few minutes, Mr. Torant's facial expression changed, like he was thinking. The two stood looking at one another, but not speaking. Then Mr. Torant began talking again, not only to my mother, but my father as well. My mother stepped off to the side, so Mr. Torant could see my father. Then my father stood up and the two shook hands. Mr. Torant placed a hand on my mother's shoulder and spoke. My mother nodded her head, as if of approval. Afterwards, Mr. Torant walked off, and my mother took her seat.

Duffers really came out throwing hard. He was an exceptional reliever, a rare trait in 17 year olds according to Cavanaugh. Duffers could throw as hard as anyone in the state for 3 maybe 4 innings, and then it was as if his arm just dissolved. Cavanaugh spotted his talent right off and knew just how to make the most of it. A good reliever is a starting pitcher's best friend, Cavanaugh always told me and Roly.

Duffers retired the side easily, allowing no base hits, and the Bulldogs were back at the plate.

Manny led off the inning with a walk, and stole second base on the next pitch. We were running all over them. The Moore's Creek coach stepped onto the field; threw his hands up in the air and snatched his hat off his head. "Jesus," he yelled.

Manny had beaten the throw by more than two seconds, and stood smiling on second base. He reached into the neck line of his jersey and pulled his gold chain back out. He had it tucked away for the stolen base effort. With the widest grin I had ever seen, white teeth glaring all the way to the outfield, Manny jumped up and down on the bag, and said:

"Hey Coach. We might need to get a new bag out here. This one's gettin' kind of flat from all the usage."

Our dugout was rolling. The Moore's Creek coach

wrung his hat in his hands, kicked the dirt, and resigned to his dugout.

Three girls stood up in the bleachers and cheered Manny's name in unison. I rolled over on the ground and stared up at the sky, laughing all the while.

Fitz singled up the middle and O'Conner got all of a fastball and sent it to the left field fence. He cleared the bases, and stood smiling on second base.

"I think you're right, Manny," Cole said, hopping up and down on second base. "There's not much spring left is there?"

The rest is history. The Bulldogs scored a few more runs, and had an expressive time doing it. If there was ever a chance to see Cavanaugh smile, it would have been that night. But he stood stoic, as he always did. It was one of the finest displays I had ever seen from my teammates. In just the last two innings, they managed to crush the Moore's Creek Panthers 14-9.

The last out of the game came by way of a grounder to Miller at second base. He tossed the ball to Godfrey, and the game was over. The Hillcrest Bulldogs were victorious; once again against the odds.

The two teams lined up and shook hands with one another. The Moore's Creek coach never came out of the dugout. Cavanaugh, in gentleman fashion, walked to their dugout and extended his hand to the losing coach. The man begrudgingly returned the gesture.

My teammates were going wild in the dugout, but Cavanaugh put an end to it quickly. I couldn't hear him, but I knew what he was saying: "Never revel in front of an opponent." He always said it. I was certain Manny and

Cole were reprimanded for their shenanigans on second base. That type of behavior was not acceptable to our coach. It never had been and it never would be.

He sat them all down and spoke for a few minutes. I would have given my left foot to hear what he said to them, because when he was through, the entire team, together, bolted out of the dugout in a sprint. In one long, blurred streak they crossed the infield, the outfield, and disappeared through the gate at the distant end.

The parents, the scouts, the newspaper reporters, and the television crews that were waiting, would not speak to the members of the Hillcrest Bulldogs tonight. Only Cavanaugh remained on the field.

The scene caused an emotion in me that I had never felt. I was envious of something that I had once been a part of. I was jealous of the feelings that my teammates were now experiencing without me. I was a part of nothing. What I had made my family, what I had made my life, what I thought I was a crucial part of, was just as strong without me. All that I had worked for, all the years I had spent training for a night like tonight, was for naught. Whatever rewards I had reaped during the game were gone. I lay in the darkness, looking at shadowy figures moving under the bright lights of a baseball stadium, and was simply forgotten.

I stayed in my spot until everyone was gone. I contemplated my plight, realizing that sooner or later I would have to face a great number of things.

Chapter 21

WHEN EVERYONE WAS GONE I climbed the fence and walked across the outfield. Crossing the infield I couldn't help but to stand on second base. Manny and Cole were right: it had gotten a lot of wear. The bag was smashed down almost flat.

The stadium lights were still on. They were humming in my ears. The place was empty and quiet. I walked to the dugout and stood staring at the empty bench. I noticed a baseball that had rolled underneath; Cavanaugh must not have seen it, I thought, as I walked down the steps into the dugout.

I picked up the ball and took a seat on the bench. I don't know how long I sat there. It may have been hours or maybe only minutes. Cavanaugh was gone, my friends were gone, the fans and all the families were gone. It was a different place when I was here alone. Without the chatter, the action, the cheering, without the game, it was a totally different place—just a field, a grass infield, dirt around the bases, and a chain link fence surrounding it all.

I got up and walked out to the pitcher's mound. Nothing was ever as easy as throwing a baseball, and I wished it were. In my mind I had mastered the game, like a martial artist flowing through the movements of a kata, like water over rocks, unimpeded and unhindered.

I stood on the mound and thought long and hard. This has been my life for a long time, I thought. I have cared about nothing else except this game, and it is the only thing I am good at because of it. My mother is right—I walk around the house and don't say anything to anyone; just me and that damn dog. 'Who do I think I am?' She says to me. I am Corey Wails, and I only know how to do one thing—throw a baseball really hard.

I was confused. Where had things gone so badly? All these years I have blamed everything on my mother, and she must have been blaming them on me. But it's not a matter of blame now, it's a matter of moving past it.

I looked down at home plate and saw a white pentagon nailed down in the dirt. I wound up and threw the ball as hard as I could at the backstop. It hit with a loud thud, and fell to the ground. I need to learn to do something else, I thought. Baseball is not going to solve my problems or answer my questions.

When I started off the mound and back across the infield, I noticed someone in the stands. I thought I was alone. I looked at the parking lot; there was only one car there and it belonged to my mother. She walked through the gate, onto the field, and headed towards the backstop where the ball was lying. She bent down and picked it up. She turned it over in her hand as if she knew what she was holding.

"So, this is where you spend all your time," she said in a pleasant voice.

"This is it," I answered.

"You know my father loved baseball the way you do," she said. "He used to take us to Memorial Stadium when I was just a little girl. Girls couldn't play baseball back then, but I sure wanted to. I knew I would have been better than the all the boys," she said in a calm, relaxed way. "Let's see if I remember how this goes," she continued, cocked her arm, and threw me a line drive.

"Wow, that was impressive," I said, as I caught it.

My mother crossed the infield and came to where I was standing. I felt terrible about this morning, especially now, but I knew it would never be mentioned again. It was one of those things I would have to live with silently for the rest of my life.

"I used to play catch with your grandfather all the time," she said, and I noticed her smile. I had not seen it in a long time and I wondered what in the world she had to smile about now. "Corey, I wish I could be as good of a mother as I was a daughter," she said, taking the ball from my hand.

"Yes Ma'am," I answered.

"I have been thinking about my father a lot lately. He would be ashamed of me if he knew how things are between us. I'm almost glad he isn't here to see it," she said. "We had arguments and he stood his ground like he should have, but I always knew he was only looking out for my best interests. I listened to him, and I respected him. And after he died I learned even more from his lessons—all the things I didn't learn the first time around. Anyway, I have something I want to share with you; something I think you will find invaluable later in life when you walk the same path as me."

I gave my mother time to collect her thoughts. I saw her struggling with her emotions. The way she passed the ball back and forth between her hands restlessly, the way she paused between her words, and between her thoughts, were all telling.

"I know I haven't been a very good mother ..."

"Mom, it's not your fault. It's just as much mine."

"Corey, just listen please," she said evenly. Her eyes were determined. "I have made mistakes, and I am sorry for that. It's normal for children not to get along with their parents, but we have moved beyond that. I have known it for years, but have done nothing about it. Time may have worked things out between us, but we don't have that option now. It is now or never son. When I am gone, trust me, you will regret not using this time wisely. Do you understand what I am trying to tell you, and just how important it is?" she said.

"Yes Ma'am—you are going to die soon aren't you?" I said, wiping tears from my eyes.

"Yes. Sooner than I would like," my mother replied, her eyes sharp.

She placed the baseball back in my hand, and grabbed my free hand with hers. "I've read about people's dying wishes coming true and I feel lucky to be able to stand here and tell you mine," she said. "Corey, I want you to remember me like I used to be, not like I have become. I want us to be friends, and I want to die knowing that you love me."

I could not believe the things she was saying or from where this person had reappeared. She walked onto the baseball field like a shadow from the past.

"Mom, I do love you. I always have. I don't mean it when I tell you I hate you."

"Yes you do, but it's okay. I have hated myself at times. There's a fine line between the two emotions. If you didn't care at all then I would be worried," she said and put her arms around me. She pulled me tight against her body. She wasn't trembling, but in full control of her every emotion. "We'll get through this—you and I together," she said in a resolute tone.

Years worth of tears were pouring out of my eyes. Why did her life have to be the price for this long overdue talk? A talk we had put off for so long that lasted only a minute. It was too much, and my legs folded. I dropped down on the infield, and cried my heart out. My mother remained standing, rubbing my head, and talking to me softly. With my emotions bottled up for so many years they had failed to develop like my pitching arm, and I was a wreck.

I learned a new meaning, and saw a new twist in my mother's strength that night. It took a lot of courage to speak about her own death so openly, to admit her faults as my mother, and to confront me, but it took an astounding amount of strength not to cry about it. For years, she had been crying in her own way, but now she was going to appreciate the days that remained without tears. It was to our grave misfortune that it took such a catastrophe for things to change.

Chapter 22

MY FATHER was waiting for me when I got home. He rose from his chair in the living room and cut me off as I was crossing the kitchen.

"Kicked off the team, Corey ... for not getting to school on time. I can't believe you. Do you have any idea the opportunities you are going to waste because you can't get out of bed on time?" my father said sternly.

"Yes sir, I do."

"I don't think you do," he replied. "I don't blame John Torant one bit. I would have done the same thing. He told you were off the team if you were late one more time. Didn't he?"

"Yes sir," I replied.

He shook his head in disgust, and started clinching and releasing his jaw muscles. I had seen that look a thousand times; he looked like he had a piece of candy pressed against his front teeth.

"I can't believe you. Why would you do something to

jeopardize things now? Why?" he said louder.

"I don't know. I didn't mean to. The day I was late was the day mom was ..."

"Don't even say it," he said, narrowing his glance at me. "Not another word from you or I may lose my temper. Get out of here. Go somewhere where I can't see you."

I shuffled across the den, treading lightly past the giant. My mother was standing in the room with us, but had not said a word. As I headed down the hall to my bedroom, I heard her soft voice saying my father's name. I stopped at my door, and strained to hear.

"Robert," she said easily. "Let me handle this, please. Will you do that for me?"

My father made no reply.

"Let me do this for him. It will mean a lot to me. He is still learning, Robert. He's just a teenager. You remember when we were teenagers don't you?" she said.

"I never acted like he does," my father said.

"I distinctly remember a young man named Robert Wails getting kicked off the track team for stealing road signs."

"It's not the same, Linda. And you know it. I didn't have scholarships riding on it. He has the potential I never had, and he is going to waste it."

"It is the same. You just don't remember. I am asking you for a favor. Forget this ever happened and let me handle it. Will you do that for me?"

My father still made no reply.

After some time, my mother said, "Thank you."

The next morning I awoke early and got to school a half an hour early. Mr. Stewart, my first period teacher, entered the room and found only me sitting in the classroom.

"Howdy," he called out in his easy way and took a seat on his stool. He plopped a newspaper down in front of himself and took a sip of his coffee. "The papers are still giving you boys a rough time of it," he said. "I guess you'll have to win the whole dern thing to make believers out of them."

"I guess so," I said deflated.

"You think they can win it all without you," Mr. Stewart said, much to my surprise. I guessed then that everyone knew what had happened.

"No doubt about it," I answered. "Did you see the game last night? They've never played better. They don't need me."

"I wouldn't say that, but they did play a heck of a ball-game," Mr. Stewart said, and took a sip of his coffee.

He opened the sports page and sat staring at the head-lines and the photograph. He held it up and showed it to me. The headline read, 'The comeback Bulldogs rally in the 7th to up set Moore's Creek 14-9.' The picture was of Todd Manny standing on second base grinning ear to ear.

"He's one charismatic kid," Mr. Stewart said. "I'm go-ing to hate to see all you boys go. I've been a teacher for 23 years, and every year it gets easier and easier to watch kids come and go. After a while, you get to where you don't even care who you're teaching, but your class has been different. Probably because you're all so dern bad. Really makes us teachers have to work," he said with his usual sly grin. He propped a cowboy boot up on the desk in front of him and took another sip of his coffee.

"You know Wails, I agree with Torant on some things, but not everything. To me, school is a place to learn, not just what's in these books," he said and tapped his finger on the Algebra book lying on his desk. "But about life, and about people, friends, and finding your place. That's what school is about. Torant gets hung up on the rules too much if you ask me. But one thing is for sure, you are going to meet a lot of John Torant's out there," he said and pointed ambiguously at the world. "A whole lot of folks don't know any other way than to follow all the rules to a T. When you come across them, best thing to do is follow suit. I guess you're learning the hard way."

"I guess so," I replied.

"But it's not the end of the world. In his own strange way Torant believes he is doing you a favor; teaching you something now that you would learn later when the stakes may be higher."

"I don't know how they could be any higher," I said.

"Believe me, Corey. The stakes get a lot higher. This is just baseball."

The room began to fill up with students, and Mr. Stewart and I quit talking. Cole came in and took his seat next to me.

"I was wondering where you were this morning. I went by your house and didn't see your jeep. I should have known you would come early today," Cole said, sarcastically. I could tell by his tone he was pissed off at me for avoiding him the day before.

"Why didn't you tell me?" he asked "What the hell kind

of thing is that?"

"I couldn't do it. I didn't want to do anything yesterday except hide," I answered. "You guys played a great ball game," I said, changing the subject. "One of the best I've ever seen."

I noticed Cole wasn't at all surprised to learn that I had watched the game. I continued:

"The papers are still saying we're just lucky, that we don't have what it takes to go all the way."

"Maybe we don't now," Cole said flatly. "Roly can't pitch every game, and you know how Duffers is. He's only good for a few innings here and there. We need you out there."

"Naa ... if you guys play like you did last night. I mean really go after them, you can carry Roly, even if he gets tired. You guys just need to score a lot of runs for him. Give him some breathing room. There's only three more games."

"It wasn't the same out there without you. We all agreed it wasn't the same."

"It was tough to watch," I said, cutting Cole off. "What did Cavanaugh say that got you guys all fired up?" I asked.

"He said the next person he sees walking on his baseball field could take off their uniform and go sit behind the fence and watch the game with you."

Cole's words stunned me. "He knew I was out there?" I asked.

"Yeah, we all knew. Manny saw you before the game even started," Cole said. "Man, was Cavanaugh fired up. You should have heard him laying into us. He kept telling us it was his baseball field and he just let us use it. I never knew he despised walking so much," Cole said with a laugh.

"You played a great game," I said. "One for the books."

Cole agreed that the game had been one for the books.

Chapter 23

AFTER SCHOOL I headed out to the parking lot with Emily. "You can spend time with your mother now, Corey. Maybe this is the way it is meant to be," she said to me.

I just looked at her. Destiny and all that jazz wasn't something I believed in, not for a second. She had said one of those things that sounded good, and meant nothing.

"Emily, losing my spot on the baseball team is going to have lasting repercussions. I am certain of that," I said.

"You'll get through it. I have faith."

"It's going to take more than faith now," I replied. "Torant has ruined my life."

"I disagree Corey. You'll just have to work harder now."

I let her words roll by silently. The subject was moot anyway.

"Wails, I need to speak to you," a voice called out. I turned and saw John Torant standing at the edge of the parking lot.

"What the hell does he want now?" I said to Emily.

Emily turned too, and was staring at the tyrant. "He always looks like he has just eaten something bad or sour and vinegary," Emily said, grinning. "Doesn't he?"

Her comment was good for a small laugh.

"I wish he would just leave me alone," I said.

I told Emily I would see her later and reluctantly headed back towards the school. What had I done now, I thought. Nothing came to mind. I had been a role model student at Hillcrest High that day. When I was half way to him, Torant turned and started walking back to the school.

"Do you want to talk to me or not?" I called out.

"In my office, Wails," he replied sharply.

He was seated behind his desk when I entered his office. "Yes sir," I said, as I came into the room.

"Have a seat there," he said, pointing at the chair facing his desk.

"I am not usually one to go back on my word," Mr. Torant started. "Believe you me, you are a pain in my rear end, Corey Wails. I don't know why I even bother with you." He sat back in his chair considering me. All the while, I sat studying him.

John Torant was in his late forties, maybe fifty. While some said he wanted to be a police officer, his appearance was that of a banker, or an accountant, or someone who lives their life in a manila folder; he was organized in every way.

"Your mother spoke to me about this matter of ours. She is concerned. I for one do not blame her for that. She should be," he said. "I told your parents what I think of you. You are a bright young man. If you get yourself straightened out you may have a future. You're a good athlete; you are an above average student. Your teachers speak highly of you. You have plenty of friends. Your marks in school are very good. But you are insolent. You are arrogant. You show no respect to me, or any of the other administrators. This attitude of yours is to your own detriment. I tried to impress this upon your mother. And you know what she said?" he asked, wide eyed, with a grin beginning.

"No sir."

"She said, 'I know John.' Your mother is a very capable woman, Corey. It seems to me that she has the same problem I have—making you listen, making you pay attention, getting you to grow up. At any rate, I didn't bring you in here to reshape you. I've been at that task for years. I don't suppose an afternoon in my office is going to change anything. Your mother told me why you were late two mornings ago, and I've decided to grant your mother the favor she has asked of me. She has asked that I put you back on the baseball team—that is if Cavanaugh will have you back."

My face lit up with Torant's words.

"Don't get excited just yet, Wails. There's more to it than that. The same deal goes, only this time there will be no exceptions. I will take what happened 2 days ago as an anomaly at your house. Why didn't you tell me about it?" he said quickly.

"Would it have mattered?" I replied.

"That is the attitude I am talking about. It's just that type of thing that is the reason for all of this, this … conflict, for lack of a better expression, that exists between you and I. Of course it would have mattered Corey. If your mother is sick, certainly to the degree she was that day, and you had to stay and help out, then I would have made concessions. I know that things outside of our control do arise, and I would never penalize someone for something they have no control over. You could have had her call my office, or your father. Your silence in the matter is the problem here. I take that back, the 16 tardies prior to the one in the balance is the problem."

"Yes sir."

"Here are the terms of our new arrangement. You will come to school every morning at 7 AM, not 8 am, not 8:06, not 7:04. 7 AM. Do you understand me?"

"Yes sir."

"You will report to my office. Look at this as an advantage. You can use an hour of your precious time every morning to fill out college entrance forms and that sort of thing. Like I said before, you have potential, but your mother is afraid you may waste it. I have given her my word that I will do all I can for you in this regard. As for you—you need to get here one hour early every morning. In exchange, I will speak to Cavanaugh about letting you finish the season."

"Yes sir," I replied.

"Then let's go speak to your coach."

Chapter 24

CAVANAUGH was standing on the edge of the infield overseeing things. He had the team doing a drill I had never seen before. I was watching the activity in bewilderment, wondering what was going on. Everyone was moving. The assistant coach was hitting balls to the infielders and outfielders, and Parker, Jackson, and Manny were running the bases; there must have been 5 balls in the air at any one moment.

"Hit the cutoff man," Cavanaugh called out. Cole rifled the ball to Fitz, who was in shallow center field, standing with his arms and legs wide, making himself a bigger target. Jackson was rounding second base and Manny was rounding first.

"Be thinking Fitz," Cavanaugh called.

Fitz turned with the ball, and quickly threw it to third base, where Jackson was tagged out. Stoney fired the ball across the field to Godfrey at first. Parker was almost caught off guard, and stepped quickly back to the bag.

"That's what I want to see," Cavanaugh called out. "Ball games are won and lost on the base paths. Throw behind the runners, catch them unawares and tag 'em out. Take an extra base here and there on offense. They'll add up."

The assistant coach sent another ball up the middle. Fitz made a diving play, snapped the ball to Miller, and they turned a double play.

The next ball went down the third base line. Stoney fielded it, and caught Manny in a run down. Back and forth, back and forth, they reeled him in, but the last toss from Stoney had too much arc, too much hang time. Manny saw his advantage and took off towards the plate. Posie could not do a thing about it as the ball lingered. At 4 steps Manny was in a full sprint. He crossed the plate grinning.

"Excellent base running, Manny," Cavanaugh said. "Stoney, sometimes I wonder if you use your head for anything besides a hat rack. Snap the ball around, son, come on now. Do it again," Cavanaugh bellowed.

Cavanaugh had seen us walk up, but he paid us no attention. I had seen his eyes glance up, but that was all. Torant didn't intervene. He and I stood along the third base line and watched the team practice. They continued the base running drills for the better part of an hour. When they were finished, Cavanaugh lined them up at the plate and one by one he called out their names and they took off. While they ran, he coached.

"On the bases is where we're going to dominate our opponents," he said. "We're going to take extra bases, and we're going to catch them sleeping by throwing behind the runners. Am I clear?" he said.

He received a unanimous 'yes sir' from his team.

When Manny and Fitz had passed everyone, the team ran suicides until their tongues were hanging in the dirt. Finally, Cavanaugh called practice.

On their way back to the locker room, everyone on the team came by and said something to me. "Good luck," were the words said the most.

"What can I do for you, Torant," Cavanaugh said, as he walked over to the two of us.

"Ray, I have worked out a new arrangement with Wails. I am lifting my decision to take him off the team. Do you want him back?" Torant asked, cutting right to the chase.

Cavanaugh looked me up and down.

"I could use him," he replied.

"Fine. The new arrangement is that he comes to my office every morning at seven am and he will be allowed to finish the season. If he is late one more time, no excuses, he's off the team for good."

"I don't believe it'll happen again. Am I right about that, son?" Cavanaugh asked of me.

"Yes sir," I replied. "I mean no sir. It won't happen again."

"Good. Get your cleats on and start running ... until I get tired." Cavanaugh said.

It was the first time in my life that I heard Cavanaugh's command "start running" with anticipation and joy.

Cavanaugh sat in the dugout, going over the books, the records from the last game, while I ran the bases. When he got tired of watching me run the bases, I ran around the fence. When he got tired of watching me run around the fence, I ran suicides. When he was tired of that, the night was upon us. The exertion had left me empty. Not a thought lingered in my mind, only utter exhaustion. As I stood in front of my Coach, shoulders sagging, feet heavy, legs numb, heart pounding, I wanted more.

"I'll make a ballplayer out of you yet, Wails. That's enough for tonight," Cavanaugh said.

Chapter 25

I KNEW, and always had, that my mother possessed a great deal of strength, but I always thought it was a detriment not a gift. I placed my selfishness on a shelf and put my trust in my mother's words, "It's now or never, Son."

Two more weeks passed and her condition was getting worse. I watched it happening right before my eyes, like a magic trick. A cat went into the hat, and a rabbit was coming out. She got scared, and decided to have a radiation treatment.

It was a Thursday afternoon. School ended, and I headed out to the field for practice. Cole and Seth were playing catch when I walked up. We exchanged hellos and I took off running. I did not need to wait for Cavanaugh to tell me.

I was running around the field, two laps, three laps, four laps … my legs were trying to catch up to my brain. I could only think of one thing: how sad my mom looked when I left the house in the morning. I had gone back to her room and told her good-bye before leaving for school. She told me that she was going to be very sick when I got home. I wished now that I had gone to the hospital with her.

Another lap or two, and I could not take it anymore. I found Cavanaugh and asked permission to leave. He looked at me in a puzzled way, but in the end he said okay.

When I pulled into the driveway at home I noticed my father working in the yard. He was sprinkling grass seed and moving the water hoses around.

In Fayetteville, North Carolina there is a lot of infertility in the soil; sandy places where nothing will grow. My father went to great lengths to change that. He had truck loads of new soil brought in; heavy, thick, brown soil to replace the thin sandy stuff that was there, and he had the yard as finely groomed as a golf course.

There was a pile of leaves under each of the oak trees, and the burlap sack he used to pick up the leaves was hanging from a limb. I sat in my jeep for a minute watching him. There was a knot just below his ear, and just above his jaw line. He was holding his mouth in his strained, unnatural way, like he had a piece of candy pressed against his front teeth. The muscles in his face were taught as he sprinkled the new seed. Royal was following him around the yard, walking softly in the presence of a giant.

His shoulders were as broad as a barn, that's what my Grandmother always said. Somehow he was able to bear the burden of my mother's illness without a visible tear, and I wondered how. I thought about my family: human beings are not meant to be this strong. There must be a point where they break; some point where they crumble under the pressure. I did not want to be around when that day came for my father.

"What are you doing home so early?" my father asked when he saw me.

"Cavanaugh cut practice short," I lied. "How is mom?"

"She's very sick, but the doctors said the radiation treatment will help," he answered, and went back to sprinkling seed.

I headed into the house and back to my mother's room. She was coming out of the bathroom when I started down the hallway. I noticed she was limping, clutching at her side, and dragging a leg behind. She turned and looked at me.

"Hey Corey, why are you home so early?" she asked.

"I couldn't play baseball today. I was worried about you."

"I am doing OK," she said in a weak voice.

"How was it?" I asked.

"Awful. I have been so sick all day. They gave me a handful of pills to help with the nausea, but they're not working too well." She faked a smile and sat down slowly on the edge of the bed.

I sat down beside her and reached for her hand. The windows were open and the curtains drawn back on the side facing the yard where my father was working. My mother was watching him. Her books were closed and lying on the floor. She was not reading today.

"Corey, you and your father need to stick together," she said. "You are going to need each other."

"What do you mean, Mom?"

"When I die it is going to be hard on him," she said.

"He keeps everything inside, all bottled up, and one of these days the flood gates are going to open. I used to be that way. I was that strong once, but all of this has changed me. It has showed me that what I thought was being strong was really being weak. I've never confronted anything. I've just tried to hide from it, and let the days go by. I regret it now."

"Like what, Mom?"

"There are too many things ... not finishing college, not doing anything with my life. I'm just a dreamer. I could have been a better wife. I could have been a better mother. Your father works so hard to give us what we have, and I just complain that it's not enough. And with you. I never should have let things progress the way they did. But I'm still learning ...at least we didn't wait too long." A faint smile crossed her face, and she continued. "Corey, don't ever let anyone tell you it's too late. It's never too late. And don't let anyone tell you that you can't do something. I wish I had never listened to the people who told me I was too old to go back to school. If some miracle was to happen and I could live, I would go back to school tomorrow and finish what I started 18 years ago. I would go to all the places I dream about. I would be a better wife and a better mother. I would be a different person. I guess at 38 years old I am finally learning what it means to live. It's ironic that this is what it took."

"I'm sorry, Mom."

"It certainly isn't your fault, Corey. I just hope you're going to be all right without me."

"I will. I'll be fine," I answered, only because it seemed like the best thing to say to make her feel better. I didn't have a clue.

We sat in silence for a long time; where seconds seem like hours.

"Look at your father," my mother said with sharp criticism. Every action in the Wail's house was under a microscope; every detail, every miniscule detail, was becoming monumental.

After sprinkling the new seed, my father filled a trashcan with pinecones and sticks. As he was putting the trash can back into the shed, the lid caught an exposed hinge. My mother and I heard him say a few choice words, and watched him yank the trash can out into the yard. In Robert Wail's fashion he went to work on the shed. That clasp would only get in his way once. His world was far too organized for something to be in the way of progress. He hurried off, came back quickly with a toolbox, and started removing the door.

"That man is just like his father ... a spitting image," my mother said. "He's the most stubborn man I've ever met. He has been working since the minute we got home. He can't sit still. He never has."

I didn't know if now was the right time or not, but I felt like I owed her an apology. I told her I was sorry for all the mean things I had said and done. I told her that most of the time I did them on purpose, just to make her mad. She looked at me with her big brown eyes, and smiled; not a strained smile like before, but one that rose in earnest from within. She put her hand on my cheek.

"It's OK, honey. I was a kid once too, you know. It's all part of growing up. I'm the one that should have done something about it, but I didn't know how. It's funny how you see things twenty-twenty in hindsight. When I look back at my life, I see all the years I have spent crying about all the bad things that have happened to me, and realize that I have wasted the time I had to appreciate the good things, like you and your father. It seems so stupid now. I already used my one wish, but if I had two, I would ask for just a couple of years back. It seems like such a small thing to ask for, doesn't it? Just two more years to live differently—today at the cancer clinic I watched the people come and go. They looked like ghosts, like the walking dead. I'm glad you were not there to see it, Corey. What I saw was terrible and that is what I am going to look like and soon. I am never going back there. I am not having any more treatments. And after seeing what I saw today, I want to take every mirror out of this house so when I look like that, I won't know it."

Chapter 26

AFTER BASEBALL PRACTICE I started coming straight home. We ate dinner like a family should. My mother cooked when she had the energy, and we sat together long after we were finished eating. I learned things about her brother and sister, her mother, and her father. I learned about her childhood, her high school days, and how she met my father.

I sat and listened to a woman who could remember every detail of a sled ride that happened thirty years ago. She told me stories about when I was just a little kid; rubbing applesauce on my bald head, eating a bottle cap and getting rushed to the hospital, getting a wart when a toad peed on me. We spent hours talking about memories, and I had no idea I was making new ones in the process; days I would remember for the rest of my life. While my life was taking a new form, hers was coming to an end and she was remembering every last inch of it. She told me that with death in sight life seemed like just one day.

"How's mom today?" I asked my father when I entered the house.

"She has some bad news to tell you," he answered solemnly.

I walked back to my mother's room. The long hallway was dark, except for a small ray of light coming from the lamp at the end.

I found her reading Bob Marley's biography, "Catch a Fire." It was a present from me, and one she was enjoying tremendously. His plight with terminal cancer at the age of thirty-one was something she could relate to and understand. She was enjoying his story, his tales, and understanding his fear of dying.

She reached her hand out for mine, looked back at her book, marked the page, and placed it face down on the bedside table. She told me a story about Cedella Booker, Bob Marley's mother, and a song Bob Marley had written for her. 'Touch me yam, won't you touch me potato, please, mister mister …' she said, halfway singing the words. She told me it was a song about Bob Marley and his mother going to the market together to pick out vegetables from the stands. Despite the fact that she was telling me a story, there was very little emotion in her words. Her eyes were glazed, and her thoughts seemingly abstract. I knew something very bad was coming.

"Sit down son," she said in a resolute voice.

It was scaring me to see a woman who had always exuded strength to be so docile.

"Yes Ma'am," I said, and took a seat on the bed beside her.

"Things are going to get worse now. The doctors told me today that my white blood cell count is getting very low.

The cancer cells are replacing healthy ones," she said, as if recording a patient's diagnosis into a tape recorder.

"What does that mean?" I asked.

"It means that my body has been fighting until now, but the cancer is starting to get a stronger hold. White blood cells are what we use to fight off infections and disease, and I have fewer than I need now," she replied.

"Can't they do anything?" I asked.

"I can have more radiation and chemotherapy treatments, but the doctors say it will only extend my life a month or two, and make me even sicker than I already am."

"A month or two? You mean they have told you …," I stammered, "when you are going to die."

She squeezed my hand, as I struggled to finish my thought.

"Yes, they told me today," she said. "I have two months, maybe less."

It didn't seem fair and it didn't seem right. Why her and why me? I buried my head in the pillow and tried not to cry. I knew I would need those tears later.

"Corey, it's going to be OK. You are going to do just fine," my mother said consolingly, referring to her own death. She might as well have been speaking in Cyrillic. I leaned on her and put my arms around her neck. She pushed me back so I could see straight into her eyes, and said, "I'm sorry, Corey," and tears ran down her cheeks.

"What are we going to do, Mom? What am I going to do?" My head was spinning. So many things were going on in my brain. One thought barely finished before another began.

"You are going to be fine. I am going to make sure of it," she said in a calm voice. "That's my job now."

"How?" I asked.

"I don't know yet, but I am searching for the strength to be your mother, if only for these last months. Maybe this is what I'm getting for being such a bad mother," she said.

"Don't say that. Please don't say that again. It's just as much my fault as it is yours."

I hugged her and wished more than anything in the world that there was something I could do for her. She was crying, but not very hard, and not for very long.

She pushed me away, so she could look at me, and said, "I want to stay at home. I want to be here the whole time."

"Alright," I answered, with no idea to what I was agreeing. It seems I made a dual pact that night: one with the devil and one with an angel.

"I am scared," she said, and sounded like a little girl. I looked away from her. She was too sad to look at. I lay in the bed beside her, but we were silent. There was nothing to say. The doctors had stamped an expiration date on her life.

I stared at the ceiling, listening to the curtains flap every time the fan came around. The plastic cap at the end of the string was rapping on the windowsill. I could hear the cars going by on the road behind our house, and wished they would stop. The whole world should stop for this, but I knew it was not going to. When the nine changed to a ten, nine fifty-nine went to ten o'clock. The numbers on the clock display changed slowly, as if time had been altered, as if time had stopped for one brief second. The bulb in the bedside lamp popped; the light faded and left the room. It was dark, save the green, neon glow of a clock.

My mother was moving her hand around mine slowly and methodically. It made her feel better to know she was not alone, and just my hands told her so. She was thinking so hard I could feel it. Her hands were clammy.

"I can see my whole life right in front of me, Corey. I have done nothing but remember ever since the doctor told me how long I have to live. My whole life—thirty-eight years—I have seen it all in one day. Everything is happening at once."

"I can see my room when I was a little girl; the way the light splintered through the shutters. I can smell the whiskey on Pop's breath. I can hear my mother calling us for supper. I can feel the cool water from the creek on my feet; the banging of wind chimes on the porch, and the smell of angel's breath on my wedding veil—everything."

I sat morosely quiet. Her words evaded me. Her thoughts were not something I could understand. My whole life really was in front of me, but my mother was just holding hers there.

That night was the first of nights that I will remember forever. My mother's thoughts, as intense as they were, ran not only through her veins, but through mine as well. That night she took me on a dream of her own:

It looked like a giant was pulling at the ends of a cotton ball, stretching the white fiber across the sky, and over the tops of the Blue Ridge Mountains. The bird feeders were full; Blue Jays and Cardinals battling for the best spot. There were hay bails in the fields, and the smell of fresh paint on the neighbor's fence.

Two children came bursting through the front door of a farmhouse. A woman with very long hair and a pretty face called after them, "Be back at this house for supper."

By the looks of the children they were siblings, as they both had the same nose. The littlest one, the boy, was yelling for his sister to wait for him, which she did not. The mother stood in the doorway wiping her hands on her apron, and smiling.

The dirt path through the woods was shiny; small pieces of quartzite sparkling in the sun. A strong breeze started the trees swaying. The swishing sound of oak leaves mingled with the high and low pitches of the fat and skinny tubes of a wind chime.

It was a hot day and the two children spent most of it lying on the rocks in the shade, feet dangling in the cool water. The little girl impressed her brother with all her knowledge. She told him that caterpillars turn into butterflies, and tadpoles into frogs, and that frogs live forever, and butterflies for only a day. The little girl smiled hard at the thought, and splashed her feet in the water.

"You'll be a toad Davey, and I'll be a butterfly," the girl said.

"Nuh Uhh Linda. You're lying," the boy replied.

Chapter 27

THE FOLLOWING AFTERNOON I drove to Emily's house after school. It was the night of the third game of the playoffs. Game time was 7 PM, so I had some time to spare.

In the beginning, Emily would come by and see my mother often, but as things progressed she came to my house less and less. I couldn't blame her. Watching my mother's sickness run its course was not something anyone wanted to see of their own will. I guess at times I didn't see the deterioration at all; like a parent watching their children grow taller—without marks on the wall they would never notice. I tried hard not to make any marks on the wall. But I saw what no one else did: the sharpness of her mind, the acuteness of her senses, the infusion of wisdom that came with the news of her terminal illness.

Perhaps the treasure of our own mortality lies in the wisdom we are granted in death; insight into the life we leave behind. Such irony, I thought. To glance beyond what is our life, and look back at that which was. There is hardly a resemblance.

Emily was waiting on her porch for me when I got to her house. She was sitting on the swing rocking back and forth.

Emily Vallent. I said her name to myself before getting out of my jeep. I sat behind the wheel staring at her, thinking about all she meant to me. She was the glue that held me together at times; her gentle way with me, her soft kisses, and calming touch.

Royal was dying to get out of the jeep, but he was waiting for me to lead the way. After some time he decided he couldn't take it anymore. He bolted across my lap, hit the steering wheel with his rump and dove to the ground. He darted up to the porch and into the swing with Emily.

"Jesus, what was that all about," I said with a grin. "I guess somebody's happy to see you."

Emily was holding either side of Royal's face, with her hands behind his ears, taunting him, as he tried desperately to lick her face.

"I've missed him too," Emily said. "How's your mom?"

"She's doing ok," I replied, and stepped down from my jeep.

As I was walking up to the porch, Mrs. Vallent came through the front door.

"How is Linda, Corey?" she asked in a concerned voice. "I've been meaning to get over there—is she having a lot of visitors?"

"Sort of," I said. "When she feels good enough. Some days she doesn't have the energy for it. But she is doing all right."

I stood on the stoop of the porch looking up at Emily and her mother. It was amazing to me how much they looked alike. Mrs. Vallent was an attractive woman; shoulder length blond hair, and big round, blue eyes. Her features were not angled, not strong like my mother's, but soft and gentle.

Mrs. Vallent sat down on the swing next to Emily and patted the seat for me to come sit down.

"There's room, Corey. Come on and sit down," Mrs. Vallent said softly.

Emily pulled Royal into her lap and the four of us sat on the porch swing together.

"Tell me about your mother, Corey," Mrs. Vallent said, never one to hide what she was thinking.

"What do you mean?"

"I mean tell me what the doctors are saying. Your mother won't tell anyone what is going on. At the game the other night she said it was just a matter of time before she is well again. Is that true?" Mrs. Vallent asked.

"Mom, you can't ask Corey something like that," Emily said, shocked that her mom was so forthright.

"No, it's not true," I said evenly. "She is going to die and there are no ifs about it. She is not having treatment, and she is not going to the hospital."

Mrs. Vallent soaked up my words before replying. "Why Corey? Why is she not treating it?"

"The doctors told her there is no chance. They said treatment would only extend her life a few months and make her sicker than she already is."

"How are you doing? I mean how are you taking all of this?"

"I'm doing all right," I said.

"It seems a shame to me. I for one think she should take advantage of the good medicine that is out there. Will she not consider it?"

"There is nothing they can do."

"Mom, Corey has to leave for his game shortly. Will you let us talk for a minute?" Emily said.

"Oh, of course. I'm sorry. I didn't mean to interrupt," Mrs. Vallent said and got up from the swing.

"Corey, tell your mother that she is in my prayers. I will stop by next week to see her."

As Mrs. Vallent was going back into the house, she turned and asked: "What do you and your father like to eat? I'll make you something."

"Fried chicken," I replied in the best voice I could find at present.

"Fried chicken it is then," Mrs. Vallent said, returning my grin. "You're a special young man. I am sure your mother appreciates everything you are doing for her. Don't you forget that."

"Thank you Mrs. Vallent."

When Mrs. Vallent stepped inside, Emily slid Royal off her lap and turned to me. "What you just said about this time being so great between you and your mom brought tears to my eyes. You're growing up, Corey. You don't act at all like you used to."

"What does that mean? I used to act bad or something?" I said, puzzled by Emily's comment.

"No, not that. It's just that before you acted like you didn't care about anything. You didn't care about anyone else's feelings or how the things you said or did effected them. You were always so driven to practice, practice, practice, like baseball made the world go around. I mean, think about where you would be right now if all of this wasn't going on. You wouldn't be sitting on a porch swing with me before a game."

"You're right. I am changing. I am seeing the world through my mother's eyes right now—and it's a different place. Her perspective is one that I don't understand, but I'm trying. You wouldn't believe some of the things she says,"

"Like what?"

"The other day we were sitting together on the edge of the bed. We had just walked down the hall and back for her exercise, so she was exhausted. She was staring off into space with a glazed look in her eyes. She told me that she could remember every day of her life. Not only remember it, but see it, and smell it, and practically touch it. She told me that in the sight of dying, she can see clearly what all the right decisions in her life should have been, and all the things she could have done, but didn't. But she isn't regretful anymore, only relieved to at least see it before it's too late. She says the feeling is weightless."

"Is she not scared?" Emily asked.

"Some days she is, but other days she acts like nothing is the matter. It's the craziest thing I have ever seen. How she can be so strong about all of this is beyond me."

"I think the same thing about you. I would be crying nonstop if my …"

Emily didn't finish her sentence. She saw my lips quivering, and my hands pulling at my jeans. She came closer and put her arms around me. I felt a weakness inside of me that I didn't want to share with anyone.

"Come here, boy," I called to Royal, who immediately jumped up on the swing. I buried my hands in his thick coat.

"You said I was changing. And you're right about that. My mother may not be scared, or if she is, she is doing a good job of hiding it, but I am. I don't know if there is enough time to make things up to her. My conscience is eating away at me. I was terrible to her for years," I said, and kept rubbing Royal's coat. "She didn't deserve it."

"That is all behind you now. Your mother knows that. She feels the same way you do. You've been talking about all the amazing things she says to you. Well, you want to know what she said to me?"

I stopped petting Royal and looked up at Emily. "What?" I asked.

A few tears were rolling down Emily's cheek. She reached up and wiped them away. "The day you told me about your mom, and I left school in such a hurry—I went to your house. Your mother was very upset when I got there. She told me what happened that morning."

"She told you about that," I said in disbelief.

"She said that morning marked the end of the way things used to be between you two. She told me about a dream she had, where a man was standing at the edge of a long field. He was holding a pocket watch, looking at it, and looking up at her. She said she has dreamed the same thing over and over, ever since the doctors told her the bad news. Your mother said she named the man in her dream the time keeper. She told me that for the first time in her life she realized just what time meant. She said she saw it as a reality, something that could be measured and something that could run out. She said that only one thing was important to her now, and that was you.

"Your mother asked me a strange question, Corey," Emily said. She sat very still, considering my emotions. She looked away for a second and collected herself.

"Your mother asked me if I thought you loved her."

I made no reply.

"I told her exactly what you told me that night at my house. About you wanting to shake her and tell her to wake up. Your mother said she has been thinking the same thing about you."

Chapter 28

"**I**N 1969, AN UNLIKELY GROUP OF MEN took the field for the World Series. The papers said those men had no right to share a ball park with the glorious Baltimore Orioles; they said those men weren't cut from the same cloth as the Baltimore Orioles; they said it was a miracle the New York Mets ever made it to the World Series at all; they said it was the worst ball club in the history of baseball to play for the championship. I was one of those men," Cavanaugh said.

"We didn't ignore what the papers were saying about us. No sir. We ate it up. We looked at their words. We even read the articles out loud in the locker room. Our Coach said only one thing to us before each game of the pennant race and each game of the Series. He didn't give us any long speeches, no words of wisdom, no pep talks, none of that. He just waved the newspapers in his hand, and said, 'Let's prove them wrong.'"

"Well, gentleman," Cavanaugh said, and held up a

newspaper. "The excellent sportswriters of our fair state are saying that we don't stand a chance in hell of beating Greensboro Page tonight; they're saying it was a miracle that we beat Anson County; they're saying it was sheer luck that we beat Moore's Creek. And you know what—they're still talking."

Cavanaugh gave us some time to think over his words.

"Let's prove them all wrong tonight," he said, waving the newspaper in his hand, and started through the line-up.

"Manny, you're leading off in center. Fitz, you're hitting second at short. Miller, third, at second base. Posie you're batting clean-up, behind the plate ..."

When Cavanaugh got to the number nine spot he stopped. He looked at Roly and then he looked at me. I wanted that game ball so badly I could practically feel it in my hand. He tossed the ball up in the air, plucked it from thin air, and said nothing.

After several more uncomfortable minutes, Cavanaugh called out, "It's game time. He tossed the ball in my direction and said, "Show 'em what we're made of Wails."

When the team emerged from the locker room the sun was going down into the pine trees that lined the park; a band of orange and red hovered on the horizon. The bases were whiter than normal, and the colors of our uniforms crisper in the glow of the dying sunshine. Poomf—the stadium lights came on and hundreds of halogen bulbs lit the field.

After warm-ups and the singing of the Anthem, we took the field for game three of the state playoffs.

I was standing on the back of the mound, rolling a resin ball in my hand, waiting on the first batter, when I saw my mother coming through the main gate. I watched her make her way down the path leading to the stands. She had not been out of bed in a week. Emily, Royal, and my father were walking beside her. Royal's ears were perked up, his tail was wagging, and he was smiling. My mother was smiling too. She was wearing a burgundy velvet wrap on her head, hiding the scarceness of hair. She was walking with a cane in her left hand, and my father was on her right, holding her arm, ready to catch her if she fell. She was holding her head high, her eyes were bright, and her chin up. This look of victory was something I was growing to love; this battle of hers was up and down, up and down, but tonight she was winning. She looked nothing like the ghost I left at home less than two hours ago. The look on her face was as if she were walking up the lawn to the White House.

"Let's look alive men," Coach Cavanaugh yelled from the dugout and I saw Royal's ears twitch. He knew the familiar sound of our coach's voice.

When my mother reached the stands everyone moved down and gave her the first seat on the front row. She put her cane down, leaned over, and whispered something in Royal's ear. He turned and licked her face before she could move. She smiled and rubbed her hand through his coat.

She is a powerful woman, I thought, knowing if I were in her shoes I would be lying in bed crying that my days are almost over. But if I could steal just an ounce of her strength, I thought, I could accomplish anything I wanted.

I waited on the back of the mound until we made eye contact. Her face was smooth and relaxed, not contorted with pain, and not wrinkled with worry. With an ease that struck a chord within me, my mother winked at me, as if to say, "let's put all of our worries away."

I was puzzled by my mother's change; or was it only me that was changing? I didn't need a PhD in psychology to see her transition, and her gradual acceptance of her fate. Each phase of physical decay was bringing with it a higher and higher level of consciousness, until her plight was seemingly just a consequence of life, no more and no less. I wondered intensely how such a change had occurred. By what means, and by what device had something larger than life itself crept inside the body of Linda Wails and whispered to her, "It will be OK, Linda. This is the natural way of things."

I stepped onto the mound. Mike crouched down behind the hitter and flashed two big bunny ears between his legs, the signal for a curveball.

"Jason, choke up son. Watch for the curve," the third base coach yelled to the hitter. Mike and I, grinning inwardly, watched the hitter slide his hands up on the bat. Mike shifted his weight to the outside of the plate, popped his glove open and shut, and said, "Let's see what he's got, Corey."

I threw a fastball on the outside corner. The batter couldn't have touched it with a ten foot pole.

"Stee-rike one," the umpire yelled.

"Let's play ball," Mike said, and snapped the ball back to me.

Greensboro was making solid contact with my pitches, but my fielders were playing out of their heads. Manny made a diving catch in the second. In the third, Fitz ran down a shallow fly ball to left that would have been a double for sure, and O'Conner picked off a runner trying to extend a single to a double. At the midway mark the only run scored in the game was a home run by the Greensboro catcher. He had timed a fastball perfectly and hit perhaps the furthest home run I had ever seen in our park.

"Jackson, Godfrey, Wails ..." Roly read off the order in the bottom of the sixth.

Jackson led off with a single, and Godfrey walked, which brought me to the plate with two men on base and no outs.

"Help yourself out here, Corey," Cavanaugh called from the first base line, meaning that a base hit at this juncture in the game would go a long way to help my own cause. Cavanaugh gave me some bogus signals, and I stepped into the box with the freedom to swing as I pleased. The first pitch was right down the pike with hardly any movement at all. I let it glide right by me and into the catcher's mitt.

"Stee-rike one," the umpire yelled.

Manny was in the on-deck circle, less than ten feet from me. "If there was ever a time to get a hit, Wails, this is it," he said.

I dropped down and rubbed a little dirt in my palms, and watched Cavanaugh's signals. The runners would be moving on the next pitch. The signal was on. As for me, Cavanaugh had taken the bat out of my hands. He had signaled for me to watch the next pitch; no matter where it was or how good it looked, I was not to swing.

Manny had seen the signal too. When our eyes met again, he shook his head, ever so slightly, but I noticed, reconfirming that I had read Cavanaugh's signal properly. The next pitch was perfect, right down the center of the plate again, and it took all I had not to swing at it.

"Third base, third base, third base!" the Greensboro coach was screaming, as Jackson was streaking towards the bag.

Just like Cavanaugh taught us I stayed my ground in the batter's box, standing directly between the catcher and a play at third base, forcing the catcher to step out onto the field to make a throw. The extra time allowed Jackson to beat the play.

"Interference, Ump! The batter's gotta clear out of there. Come on now ump. You gotta call it," the Greensboro coach protested.

"It's a fair play," the ump said nonchalantly.

"I'll be damned if it was," the coach retorted. "That was interference and you know it."

"That's baseball," Cavanaugh yelled across the field.

The umpire paid the coach no more of his mind, pulled his mask down, and shouted: "Let's play ball. The count is 2 strikes and no balls," and he flashed the count on his fingers.

As I stepped back into the box the catcher remarked:

"I hope you try that again, I'll hit you in the head with the ball next time."

I didn't reply. I had done my job, and I had done it right. When the commotion died down and the park grew silent in anticipation of the next pitch, I heard my mother's voice:

"Get a hit for me, son."

Any other time in my life I would have been embarrassed, but not tonight. The catcher laughed and mocked what he had heard, 'Get a hit for me, son,' he said in a high, shrill voice. "Get a hit for your mommy," he chided further.

I threw up a hand, calling for a time out, and stepped out of the batter's box. I looked down at the catcher and noticed his derisive smile coming through the cracks of his catcher's mask.

"Keep talking," I said.

The catcher stood up and pulled his mask off. The umpire stepped between the two of us, and said, "One more word out of either of you, and you're out of here."

"Come on, let's play ball," the Greensboro coach yelled.

"Wails, I don't know what's going on down there, but now's not the time," Cavanaugh said, clapped his hands together and shouted, "Let's go now."

Before I stepped back into the box, I caught a glimpse of my mother. She noticed my glance, and gently clasped her hands together in front of herself. She looked so excited just to be a part.

I stepped back into the box and took my stance. I don't know if the Greensboro pitcher was losing his steam or if he thought I didn't deserve his attention, but instead of wasting a pitch on me, he sent the third pitch right down the middle of the plate. I had seen two already, and was chomping at the bit for another. I drove a line drive to left center, bringing in Jackson and Godfrey. We took the lead, 2-1, and I stood on first base. I can count the number of base hits I ever had in high school on two hands, but that one certainly stands out.

"That's the way to help yourself," Cavanaugh said, and rapped on my helmet. "You almost looked like a hitter up there," he continued.

I was so fired up, I hardly heard his words.

"Come on Manny, keep it going," I called out, as Todd stepped up to the plate. On the next pitch I was moving; Manny laid down a bunt and beat the throw to first. Fitz and Miller both singled, and still with no outs. Our dugout was ecstatic.

That was that for the starting Greensboro pitcher. Their coach came to the mound, took the ball from his glove and brought in a reliever; a reliever who proved to be as good as our own Duffers. He retired the side easily, but the Bulldogs had gotten theirs. The score was 5-1 going into the seventh inning.

Chapter 29

AT THE TOP OF THE EIGHTH the scoreboard still read 5-1, but Greensboro had a change of heart. They came out on fire. The lead off hitter got a solid base hit. Next up was their first baseman. He drove a curveball to right field, and it was all O'Conner could do to hold a run from scoring. Next up was the catcher. He stepped into the box with an arrogant smile; one that I wanted to strip from his face.

I heard my father from the bleachers call out: "Go to work on him, Corey!"

With runners on first and third and only one out, I knew for sure Cavanaugh would call for an intentional walk, giving us a force out at any base. It was only the right thing to do, but I was dreading the call. I wanted this one to go down as a strike-out.

I looked to Cavanaugh for a decision. I could see him thinking. Up and down, up and down, he tossed the baseball. He knelt down on a knee on the top step of the dugout and said, "Go after him."

Mike moved to the inside of the plate and popped his glove with his fist. I threw a fastball on the inside of the plate. It brushed the hitter back a few steps. He turned and glared at me. I returned the gesture with a smile. Next pitch was the same thing, only this time the catcher didn't move. He stood his ground as a fastball missed his inside shoulder by only inches. The park grew quiet. The umpire didn't bother to call the pitch. Instead, he stripped off his mask, put his hands on his hips, and stood staring at me with a look of distaste. I took it as a warning, knowing if I hit this batter I would be thrown out of the game for sure.

The Greensboro catcher didn't step out of the box. His eyes remained locked on me in an intense stare. A vendetta had arisen quickly.

Mike snapped the ball back to me, shifted his weight over the center of the plate, and called for a curve.

I threw the curve Mike called for, and the catcher wasn't fooled by it. With excellent anticipation, he waited on it, waited on it, and got every last stitch. We all watched with declining spirit as the ball sailed distant of the left field fence.

"Foul ball," the umpire called at the instant the ball hooked left of the out-of-bounds marker.

The count was one strike and two balls. Mike called for another curveball, but I nodded him off. He moved his glove back to the inside of the plate and called for a change-up. I nodded him off. After another wrong call by Posie, I stepped off the mound. The Greensboro catcher remained in the box. I was beginning to think he was a statue the way he stood his ground.

I rolled the resin ball in my hand and gripped the baseball wide across the seams. Mike got the idea and positioned himself on the outside edge of the plate. I delivered a fastball with excellent precision, and the catcher made solid contact, only this time, instead of swinging early, he swung late. The ball ricocheted off our dugout fence, forcing Cavanaugh to duck back to safety as the ball slammed against the protective gate. The count was 2-2.

Still there was no change in the Greensboro catcher's demeanor. He simply pulled his bat back and readied himself for the next pitch. Mike showed me four fingers, calling for a change-up right down the pike. I didn't nod off the call. I gripped the ball for all I was worth, and with no change in my wind up, delivered what appeared to be a fastball. It was Cavanaugh, a man who had pitched in the big leagues for 11 years, who had taught me that trick. The harder you grip a baseball, the deeper you place it in your hand, and squeeze with all your might, the slower it moves when you let it fly. My arm moved like I was throwing a fastball, my body moved like I was throwing a fastball, the grimace on my face was telling of an upwelling of strength to deliver a fastball, only it wasn't. The ball moved at less than 70 miles an hour towards the plate. It seemed to never get there; it hovered, it sputtered, it moved as if I had a string attached and could yank it back at any second.

To my great disbelief the Greensboro coach called out, "Wait on it!"

That was all it took. Hitting a change-up when you know it's coming is like hitting a ball off a tee. The catcher wasn't fooled. He kept his weight back and his bat steady until the ball neared the plate. He made solid contact and sent the ball over the center field fence.

As he trotted around second base he called out, "Hey, Pitcher. That one was for your mommy."

"Don't pay him any attention," Fitz said. "There's no damage done. Just get us out of this inning."

I was livid. One wrong pitch to the wrong batter was all it took. Our lead was down to one run, 5-4. Cavanaugh didn't say a word. You win some and you lose some. The Greensboro catcher had my number; that was all. In hindsight, I should have walked him.

With no more incidences, I got us out of the inning. The Greensboro reliever shut us down again in the bottom of eighth, and the score remained 5-4 going into the ninth.

The first batter rapped on home plate, and took his stance. He had his bat in front of him, instead of tucked behind his shoulder. They were switching styles on me, like a righty boxer going to southpaw with his back on the ropes. The hitter punched the first pitch just over Fitz's head at short.

I moved into the stretch and they executed a hit and run to perfection. The batter laid down a bunt and I stumbled off the mound trying to cover it. The Greensboro dugout was doing their best to steal my nerve and I believe they accomplished it. They were rattling the fence, chanting, and clapping. Posie came to the mound and we discussed the scenario.

"Corey, this guy's been swinging late all night. Throw it by him," Mike said. "Put all their chatter out of your head and concentrate."

I stepped back on the mound and looked at the hitter in the box. I had no outs, two men on base, with a one run lead in the ninth inning. It's clutch time, I told myself.

When the batter squared around to bunt, I couldn't believe it—two in a row. Posie stood up as soon as he saw the batter's intentions. While Mike kept his cool, I had lost mine. I tried to change my pitch, midstream, and aim for his head, just like Cavanaugh taught me. I let the ball go; the batter folded like an accordion, and the ball went ninety miles an hour right over his head, and out of Mike's reach. Both runners advanced on the passed ball, and the count was one ball and no strikes, with runners on second and third. Coach Cavanaugh came to the mound.

"Son, you gotta bear down now," he said, and took the game ball from my glove. I noticed Duffers moving to the bullpen to warm up, but I knew Cavanaugh had already made up his mind that this was my game to lose. If he was going to take me out, he would have already done it.

"This is when it counts, son. They've got all the momentum. They're playing games with you now. They're stealing your nerve and rattling your cage. You need to rattle theirs."

"Yes sir," I answered.

"Send this man down to first base, and I don't mean walk him," Cavanaugh said with an intensity I had never seen. He placed the game ball back in my glove. "Do you understand me?"

"Yes sir."

I stood on the back of the mound looking at my predicament. We had no outs, with runners on second and third. I almost wished he had brought Duffers in to get us out of this mess. An intentional walk was, once again, the best thing to do, giving us a forced out at any base, but Cavanaugh was of a different mind. I knew he was right.

With the way things were going, putting a man on base the cheap way would do nothing but fuel the Greensboro fire.

I was tired from eight innings of pitching and my arm was sore. I found myself making excuses. I found my mother in the stands. She was smiling and watching me. She was leaning forward in her seat, her hands folded in her lap. I knew my father was anticipating the intentional walk, as his eyes were on the hitter in the on-deck circle. Mike got down and flapped his mitt. The batter took his stance, and with no more thought about it, I delivered a fastball straight at him. He turned his back on the ball and it struck with a thud just below his shoulder blade. The Greensboro Page dugout cleared; they stood on the third base line, livid. My outfielders, Jackson, Manny, and O'Conner rushed into the infield. Miller, Stoney, and Fitz came to the mound. Posie stayed behind the plate with his mask in his hand. I kept my eye on their catcher, knowing if chaos broke out, he would be coming for me.

"It was intentional, Ump!" the third base coach yelled.

Cavanaugh came onto the field, along with our assistant coach. The downed hitter got up from the dirt, and grabbed his bat. The stadium was in pandemonium.

"You gotta throw 'em out of the game, Ump," the Greensboro coach yelled again.

The umpire made no call.

"There'll be no such thing," Cavanaugh said. "I say when my pitcher comes out of the game."

"Leave that bat, and take your base," the umpire said to the hitter. He walked slowly down the first base line, glaring at me the whole way.

"Pitch, I'm officially warning you," the umpire yelled. He took his stance behind Posie, and called, "Batter up."

Cavanaugh was right. The event certainly changed the momentum. Rage is a hard emotion to settle, and the next two batters swung for the fence with little precision. The first hitter sent a dribbling grounder up the middle. I fielded it and tossed it to Posie at home base, forcing the runner out.

"One down, two to go," Posie yelled, holding up one finger.

The next batter grounded to Fitz at short. Fitz fielded it cleanly and tossed it to Miller. They turned a double play to end the game. Greensboro Page left the bases loaded in the ninth inning, but scored no runs. Narrowly, the Bulldogs advanced to the semifinals of the State Championship.

Words were exchanged as we lined up and slapped hands with Greensboro Page. Jackson and Godfrey were more than ready if it came to blows, but nothing came of the tension, save some words.

The Greensboro catcher didn't move from his spot in the dugout. He sat wrenching his hands, with tears in his eyes. I thought better of taunting him, and had to talk Jackson out of saying a word in his direction. I was sure that bull would have come raging onto the field. His dream had been stolen, while ours was more alive than ever.

Chapter 30

I WAS EXCITED that we won, but watching my mother leave the stadium far outweighed the pleasure of victory. While my teammates were celebrating, I watched her leaving the ballpark. She was leaning on my father with all her weight, and dragging her feet. She had used all of her strength to sit up for the game. I felt bad that she was trying so hard on my account, and just like she told me she would, she was getting sicker every day.

It was almost 10:30 by the time I got home. All the lights in the house were out, except the flickering of the living room television. My father must have heard me come in, because as I was coming through the pantry a lamp came on the living room. He sat up in the recliner. The television was turned to one of the old movie channels. In the background I heard a man saying his name was Judah Ben Hurr.

"You played a good game tonight, son. You sure picked a good time to get a base hit," he said, and strained a smile.

"Must be all those extra cuts with Cavanaugh."

"Probably so. Either that or the loud-mouthed catcher," I said. "What's the matter? Why is the house so dark?"

My father didn't reply.

"Can't you leave a porch light on, or the car port light or something? It's too dark," I said.

Still my father made no comment about the darkness.

"Look in the oven. Your mother left you something to eat," my father said. "She's still trying, but I think she realized tonight that she can't do so much. She's a lot sicker than she leads on, Corey."

"Can't anything be done? If we talked her into going back to the doctors, isn't there something they can do for her?"

"No. There isn't a thing in the world that can be done. The type of cancer she has can not be treated. We've known that all along. After you make a plate, come sit in here. I want to talk to you for a minute."

In the oven I found a baked chicken. My mother had found the energy and the will to get the meat from the freezer, remove the plastic wrap, place it on a rack in the oven, and turn the oven on. She had done nothing else. The plastic that held the leg bones together had melted all over the drumsticks. I pulled at the breast with a fork, until I had something edible on my plate. I noticed on the counter top was an unopened can of peas. Next to the can was a can opener and a small sauce pan. I guessed my mother had greater intentions, but lacked the endurance.

"You don't want any, Dad?" I asked.

"No thanks. I got something at the game."

I took my plate over and sat down on the couch.

"You made some interesting decisions out there tonight," my father said. "Did you hit the batter on purpose?"

"Yes sir."

"I guessed as much. What possessed you to throw that kid a change-up? You should have kept wasting pitches on him. A walk was a heck of a lot better than giving up a home run. You're lucky you didn't lose the game because of it."

"Hindsight is 20/20 isn't it? Had I struck him out with that pitch, you would be thinking how good of a decision it was."

"Maybe so," he said. "But I wouldn't have thrown that pitch. Not to him. He had a keen eye. Best case was to walk him, but I'm sure you know that. Anyway, what I want to talk to you about is your future. Have you thought about it? You've got letters from colleges piling up, and I haven't seen you paying attention to any of them. What about Clemson? Six months ago it was all you talked about, and now you never mention it. If you don't take the spot they've offered you, they're going to give it to someone else. Same with all the schools."

"I don't know dad. I don't know what I want anymore. As crazy as it may sound to you, I don't think I want to go to college, and I'm not sure I want to play baseball after the playoffs are over."

My father sat up quickly. "What are you saying?"

"I don't know. Going through all of this with mom is really changing my perspective. I think while I am young I need to do some exploring. I need to get out there and see the world. Baseball is all I know. There's got to be more to life than baseball."

"I'll tell you what you need to see—the inside of a university. You need to go to college and make something of yourself. And you need to use baseball to get yourself there. I can't believe my own ears. What has gotten into you?"

"I don't see what making something of my life and going to college have to do with one another."

"You will."

"Like Cavanaugh always tells us, if you're going to give less than a hundred percent, you might as well find something else to do. I don't think baseball is going to take me very far. Not anymore."

"Son, sometimes in life you have to be realistic. What Cavanaugh says is true, but it is one of those things that sounds good, but is vaguely realistic. The flip side of that is at 75% you're still good enough to go to college on a baseball scholarship. I don't think you realize how important education is. You need to get there any way you can. Later on, when you decide to go, but you're too old to play ball, your grades alone aren't going to get you into a good school."

"Maybe so, but I can't worry about everything at once. I can't worry about what-ifs down the road. Fact is, I don't think I want to go to college, and I don't think I want to play baseball. Twelve years is long enough. I'm ready for something new."

"You're just confused right now, son. Hell, so am I. But when you're thinking clearly again, you'll regret making a hasty decision. Just put some thought into it, that's all I am asking."

"Yes sir. How is mom? I watched her leaving the park."

"It's been a rough night for her. But she loved your baseball game. She was so excited when you got that base hit. I told her you did that sort of thing all the time," my father said and shot me a genuine smile. "What was that, the 4th hit you've ever gotten?" he said with a chuckle.

"Well, I need to go back and see mom," I said.

I put my dish in the kitchen and started across the living room.

"In case it comes up, I told your mother you didn't hit that batter on purpose," my father said. "And I want you to think about what we just talked about. Don't put it off."

"Yes sir."

Chapter 31

MY **MOTHER** was still awake, staring off into space when I reached her bed. I was in plain view of her, and yet she had not heard me. She usually spoke to me before I reached the end of the hall, but not tonight. She was deep in thought; thoughts that allowed no noise from the outside world to disrupt.

When she started her battle she knew it was uphill, but she had a lot of determination. As she grew sicker, fear undermined her courage, and she grew scared. I can only imagine how scared she must have been.

With a jolt, she realized I was standing there.

"I'm sorry, Mom. I should have said something. Was it a good place?" I asked.

"What do you mean?" she said, confused.

"Wherever you just were, because it wasn't here," I said with a smile, trying to make light of something.

"Oh yes. I was just remembering. It seems that's all I do anymore. I just remember."

I took a seat on the bed next to her.

"Corey, you played so good tonight," she said.

"Thanks Mom. ... But you don't have to come anymore. I know how hard it is for you now. You should save your energy for something else."

"What else is there?" she said.

She grabbed my hand and started moving her fingers softly over my skin.

"I don't want to die, Corey. Not now. Not like this." She looked at me with her big eyes, brown and pleading to anyone; anyone who could make this all go away, like it was a dream or a nightmare and someone could wake her up.

"There were so many things I wanted to do, and I never did any of them. I have never even seen the Pacific Ocean. I have never seen a desert. I have never seen the big mountains out west. I have never been anywhere. When I was little I dreamed about all kinds of things I wanted to do. My father used to tell me stories about far away places where he had been in the military. It was always so much fun to listen to him. I don't have any stories of my own, and never will. Not now."

"I will see those places for you. I promise. I dream the same as you do, and I am going to do something about it," I said.

"Don't wait like I did. Your chance may never come. When I think about all of this, it doesn't even seem real. I can't believe that I am lying here dying. I am thirty-eight years old. It just can't be."

"Maybe you will get better. There is always a chance, isn't there?"

"No, Corey. Look at me. You need to accept it now. There is no chance that I will survive. There is no chance that I will be here next year, probably not even next month," she said and her jaw tightened.

I moved closer and put my arms around her neck. "I don't know what I'm going to do without you," I said.

"You will be fine son. I have to believe that ... everything happens for a reason, honey. It's up to you to figure out where the good is. If I've only learned one thing through all of this, that's it, and I want you to remember that."

"What could possibly be good about this, Mom?" I asked.

"That's something only you can answer," she replied.

We laid there in silence for a long time. I could feel my mother's worry, so I decided to tell her a funny story, thinking maybe it would make her feel better, or at least make her smile.

"Did I ever tell you about the time Granddaddy and I were scooping up groundhog holes in the front field?" I asked.

"I don't think so," my mother said, shifted her body towards me, and put her head back on the pillow. She liked listening to my stories almost as much as I liked telling them.

"I was probably eight years old. Granddaddy was walking behind the tractor with the horse plow. You know the big scoop we use to dig up potatoes," I said.

"I know what a horse plow is, son," she replied emphatically; her tone reminding me that she had lived her whole life on the farm before I was born.

"We were at the top of the hill in the front lot, right

next to the black walnut tree. You know where I am talking about?"

"Yeah, on the right side of the road coming up to the
farm. That's a big hill," she said.

"Yeah, that's the hill. It was so steep that if we had the
wagon full of hay we had to go around it … I was driving
and Granddaddy was holding the handles of the plow up
over his head and the scoop was shaking and jumping out
of the ground. He was yelling 'whoa' and 'come on boy'
and the plow was leveling off the groundhog den. When
we crested the hill, he said 'whoa', and do you know what
I did?"

I gave her some time to think about it, but she made
no guess.

"Right at the top of that huge hill I pushed the clutch
in. Granddaddy always told me the clutch makes the
tractor stop. He never bothered to tell me only if you're
not on a hill."

My mother started laughing.

"We tore down that hill as fast as the wheels would turn
on the tractor. You think you've heard Gene Wails cuss?
You should have heard him that day. He was bouncing up
and down as I drug him all the way to the bottom. I froze
up with my foot pressing the clutch as hard as I could.
He was belted into the harness so he couldn't let go. In
between a few of his curse words, I heard him tell me to
take my damn foot off the clutch. When I did, the tractor
stopped on a dime. I almost went over the steering wheel,
and Granddaddy's head hit the scoop and he cut his forehead wide open. He didn't even go to the house. We went
straight to the barn, and he worked on the mill the rest of

the day holding an old, dirty rag on his forehead."

My story had the desired effect and she was grinning ear to ear.

Chapter 32

AT THE POINT WHERE MY MOTHER could no longer walk or do anything at all for herself I quit school. I worked out an arrangement with the principal to have my assignments brought to me at the end of each day and I only left the house in the afternoon to attend baseball practice and the remaining games of the State Championship.

My life at home took on a whole new meaning. I felt like I was a part of something, something larger than myself or my mother—something larger than life itself. I was changing from a wide-eyed, bewildered boy who dreamed of little else other than baseball, into the man I would someday become.

She had moments of lucidity followed by periods of detachment, where the world fell away from her leaving her suspended in white fluffy clouds riding them to Heaven, or bound to a stake in a place that resembled Hell; a place not even her dreams could make real for me without the intense pain that brought her visions to life.

She lay in bed twenty-four hours a day, pondering her own death and struggling to form an alliance between herself and her creator. Her waking dreams and vivid illusions told her there were two places she may journey in the hereafter, and the one full of pain was not a place she wanted to spend eternity.

During her last days on Earth, Linda Wails became a Christian; a moment marked by the minister of her church. With her sins behind her, she entered the family of God's children, beating frail and damaged wings in a strong wind; a brief moment in time, but a moment that made the remaining ones pass easier. She believed not in the existence of a god, but in God Himself with all her heart and soul. She found salvation in something I could not see, could not feel, and could not understand.

We spent hour upon hour sitting in her room talking about our lives together. How terrible it had been at times, and looking back, how easily we could have rectified our differences. She talked to me about her father's death and the difficult time she had coping with it. She knew intimately how terrible it is to have things left unsaid, feelings locked inside forever, and never shared with a person now unreachable.

She wondered if she had ever told her father how much he meant to her, if she had met the requirements of a good daughter before his death. There was no time for preparation by the family, a fortune that was granted my mother and I, and one we used to its fullest. Her remaining days were some of the most rewarding of my life and ones that I would never forget; days that formed the convictions I would hold for the rest of my life.

It was late in the morning when I walked back to my mother's room to check on her. She was wide awake and reading her bible, a recent gift from her minister. Her eyes were wide-open, lips coated with a pink gloss, and the color back in her cheeks. She had the appearance of health. The resiliency of the human body never ceased to amaze me. I saw death as a burglar sneaking in and out, and today it was gone.

My mother seemed happy and content. The strong mind-altering medication had worn off and she was enjoying a reprieve from both pain and clouded thoughts. Her face almost had a smile on it. She had the look of a person on vacation in a strange but comfortable bed, taking advantage of waking up late and enjoying a good book. The only thing that was out of place was the decorative hat she wore to cover the few strands of hair that remained on her head.

"Hey, son," she said, and placed her book down. It was a pleasure to see her free of pain, at least for a little while. "Will you take me to the bathroom please? I want to shower today."

It was so much effort for her to get out of bed, that something as strenuous as a shower had to wait until she felt strong enough.

I went to the bathroom and got things ready. In the shower, I placed the chair with rubber stoppers on the legs. She was not able to stand, but could sit in the chair and let the water run down her body. Breathing was such a chore that a full stream of water over her mouth was too much for her. But there was something ethereal about the water; something that lifted her spirits and provided a period of safety and comfort, if not physically, spiritually. She told me so.

When I returned to the bedroom, the bed covers were turned down; exposing what was left of her legs and hips. Her silk pajamas clung to her skin like Saran wrap.

"Are you ready?" I asked and she nodded approval. She took a deep breath in preparation. I bent over and carefully placed my left arm under her bent knees, and moved my arm up until I could feel the limp weight of her legs. She made a sound as the pain escaped her mouth, and leaned forward to allow my other arm to go behind her back.

"Ok, here we go," I said.

I lifted my arms, straightened my back, and lifted her off the bed. She let out a long sigh as I stood up. Physically, I got used to the task of carrying my bedridden mother from the prison she was confined to, but emotionally, the task grew harder every time. My stomach knotted when I felt her bony legs against my forearms, and the loose skin that was once taut around her muscles, that now hung from her bones.

My right arm ran the distance of her back and my hand grasped her right shoulder firmly. It felt like the knobby protrusion at the end of a baseball bat. I could feel the hard edges of her rib cage pressing against my arm. She held her chin down as her neck strained to support the weight of her head. When the sigh was complete, I knew she had fought through the pain of being moved and was ready for me to take her to the bathroom.

There were times when being lifted off the bed was too much and she had to pass up the water that made her feel better, but today she was going to make it. I carried her down the hallway and noticed her head come up just enough to look at the pictures on the wall.

"Stop," she said, as we were passing by the first collage of photographs. She stared at the pictures for a moment but said nothing. She was staring at a picture of her father, dressed in a military uniform, standing in the top of a tall palm tree. He was a young man; the picture taken before my mother was born.

Her eyes scanned all the pictures in the collage. I expected tears, but she was smiling. For some reason, today, she was comfortable with her plight. She had full acceptance of her situation, and had re-channeled her physical strength into a mental toughness that would see her through the nightmare that had become her life.

"Remind me to tell you a funny story about my father, Corey."

I knew she wanted to look at all the pictures; pictures she had carefully selected and had framed in collages to line the walls of her bedroom, but she lacked the endurance for such a task. I thought it would be nice to bring the pictures to her bed, and let her tell me stories about each of them.

"Do you want to take a bath instead today, Mom?" I asked, remembering when she was healthy. She enjoyed lying in the bathtub and reading. I thought it would be a good thing for her today.

"I guess I could try," she answered.

I carefully set her down on the toilet and removed the chair from its place in the tub, and started the water running, making sure it was not too hot.

"Can I brush my teeth?" she asked.

"Sure."

I looked on the counter and saw the nasty, blue, government-looking, hospital pan. The site of it pissed me off. My mother was not in the hospital, and it was the only request she had made, not to go to the hospital—ever. The blue pan shaped like a golf course hole drawn on the little map they give you at tee time remained on the counter. I grabbed a towel instead, and placed it in her lap. She put a hand on it and let her fingers feel the material. The soft material was pleasing to her; I noticed her face and shoulders relax.

I put some toothpaste on her toothbrush and handed it to her. She started moving the brush back and forth in her mouth, slowly, like someone who has not brushed their teeth in a very long time. She was enjoying the bristles on her gums and the bite of antiseptic in her mouth. I placed a cup under her and she spit into it.

"Mmmm, this feels so good," she said with a smile that engulfed the toothbrush. She was like a little kid. Once a man and twice a child, or in this case, a woman, I thought. I couldn't figure out if the way she acted was because of the medication, the cancer, or the simple fact that everything she did had a number on it and would all be over someday, and that day was soon. Whatever the reason, she enjoyed things to a much higher degree than a person who is healthy; a person whose life is still ahead of them.

When she was finished brushing her teeth I gave her a cup of water. She swished it around in her mouth and I held the cup in place for her to spit again.

"Thank you son," she said, and resumed the position: chin

down, hands folded in her lap, conserving her energy.

She leaned back on the commode and tried to pick up her left foot. It had barely cleared the floor when I supported it with my hand and pulled the satin pajama leg down. It was a sight I tried hard to put out of my memory forever. Every bone was visible and the once tanned skin was jaundice yellow with dark purple bruises. Her hips looked like a cradle that her body sat in, with no meat to protect her buttocks from the hard porcelain. I noticed she was no different than me in averting her eyes from the things that used to be her legs. Her skin was smooth, like a baby, but lacked the tightness of health. It looked like king size sheets placed on a bed half the size, with buckles and folds at the corners.

Slowly and painfully, for both of us, I put her in the bathtub. She let out a sigh of relief, as the water took the weight off her bones.

I left her alone to enjoy her bath. It had been a long time since she had been able to do anything on her own, and I had not thought to offer a bath before, so it had been a while. I went back to her bedroom, removed the sheets and put new ones in place. I found another set of the satin pajamas she liked to wear and set them to the side. I cleared all the dirty glasses away from the bedside and refilled the pitcher of water. About twenty minutes went by before she called for me.

"Can you take me back now?" she said. She still had white foam on her bald scalp and I could not help but laugh.

"Are you going back to bed with all that shampoo on your head?"

"Oh," she said, and moved her hand to feel the soapy bubbles on her scalp. She laughed too and asked me for a cup to rinse it off. She dipped it in the water a few times and poured it over her head.

"Better," she asked with a grin, looking up at me.

"That'll do," I replied.

Smiles were hard to come by these days, but she was having a great morning. It had been a long time since I had seen her enjoy anything. The unrelenting pain in her legs from bone marrow cancer, and spells of nausea had lasted for two solid weeks. But today was like the day after a long bout of rain in the fall when the sun shines through the clouds and everyone rides around town with their car windows down and their radios turned up.

I removed her from the tub as carefully as I had placed her there and carried her back to her bed. I sat her down on several towels I had laid out and helped her dry off and put her clean pajamas on. It seemed like she had a lot of strength today and I thought she might enjoy getting outside. She agreed.

I found a couple beach chairs, and placed them in the middle of the yard, in the shade of a large oak tree. I was back in a few minutes and she was still sitting in the same position, staring at the floor. The muscles in her neck were too weak to hold her head up.

"All right, let's go outside," I said as I placed my arms around her and lifted once more, not asking for consent this time. I was worried she may change her mind, and I thought going outside would be great for her today.

Chapter 33

IT WAS A BEAUTIFUL DAY. A perfect number of clouds lined the sky, making us aware of just how blue that abyss can be. It was the middle of May and the weather was just starting to warm up. As the saying goes—April showers bring May flowers—everything was in full bloom. My father had the yard in fine shape. The grass was cropped short in a diagonal pattern; each pass barely overlapping the one before. The concrete patio was lined with flower boxes full of tulips in bloom. The side of the house was covered with rose bushes, open to the spring sunshine, red in all their glory. The sloping hill at the back of the house was terraced at regular intervals with railroad ties, and dotted with pink and white dogwood trees, their blooms, the state flower of North Carolina. Two bird feeders hung on the back porch and hummingbirds of various colors flittered down and hovered, their long beaks reaching in and drinking the sugar water. No leaves remained on the ground from the season of death, when all had fallen from the southern oaks. My father had raked away all the remains of that season and prepared the yard for the next, the season when all would be in full bloom of life again.

A squirrel darted across the yard, scampered up a large oak tree, made his way across a branch and dove from its tip. Suspended in midair, partial wings outstretched, he sailed to another limb and crossed the yard from treetop to treetop in an instant. In the center of the yard, near my mother's chair, was a flower bed of all different types and colors of flowers. They had just started to bloom. Purple, red, and orange buds were intertwined in a floral arrangement encircled by a rock wall. It was a creation of my mother's and I saw her looking at it with keen interest, remembering a day when she had been healthy enough to work in the yard; strong enough to carry the rocks down from the hill and arrange them neatly in the circle that guarded her flowers. She was studying them, remembering each of their names, the kind of soil they liked, and the season they flowered. Many different kinds of flowers lie in the bed, but only certain ones bloomed in the spring, when sunlight is ample but not overbearing, when temperatures are brisk but not freezing. It seems there is a time and a place for everything to bloom, and a condition to be met for each.

"It's such a nice day, Corey," my mother said, looking around at the yard.

The bath and the fresh air had given her so much more strength than she had in the dark confines of her room with the musk of sickness on her clothes and skin. She seemed almost healthy again. She had the burgundy, velveteen wrap on her head. Her cheeks and eye sockets had regained color. She was holding her head up straight, and her legs were stretched out on the lawn chair. I brought her a glass of water, and sat down next to her.

"Has your father been working in the yard?" she inquired. "It looks really nice."

"Yes Ma'am. He usually does an hour or two of something every day when he gets home."

"Well, you certainly can tell," she said, and took in as big a view as she could.

"Mom, I'll be right back. I want to get you something." I had just remembered the pictures in the hallway.

I returned with all three collages, and placed one in her lap. It was the one of her father, her mother, brother, and sister. She held it in her hands, resting on her midsection. Her eyes were shiny, a sheen of water covering them. A smile crept across her face, and the memories flooded in.

"You were going to tell me a story about your father?" I said.

She swallowed the emotions that would bring tears, replaced it with gratitude for being able to remember, and began her story with a smile on her face.

"My father was sitting on the porch when Donna and I snuck out to the shed. We got some cigarettes at school and wanted to try smoking for the first time. We were in the shed, puffing away clumsily, when my dad walked through the door; Donna and I, each had a cigarette in our hand."

"How old were you?" I asked.

"Maybe thirteen or fourteen. Your aunt and I didn't know what to do. We tried to hide the cigarettes, but the shed was full of smoke, so it was no use. He just stood there for a second, and the longer he went without saying anything, the more scared we became. We knew he was thinking about what he was going to do. He had told us that no one in his house was ever going to smoke. He despised it for some reason. 'So you girls want to smoke?' he finally said. He put his hands on his hips and said, 'well, one a piece isn't gonna do it. Let's go to the store.' Your aunt and I couldn't believe it … 'One a piece isn't gonna do it.'" My mother repeated her father's words and started laughing. I could practically see the old man standing there in the shed with his hands on his hips.

"So we went to the store and waited in the car while he bought a couple packs of cigarettes. When we got home, he told us to go to the bathroom. He followed us in, closed the door, and put a towel under the crack and said, 'All right girls, smoke away.' He lit cigarette after cigarette and your aunt and I puffed on each one until we were so sick we were vomiting. Neither of us ever smoked another cigarette."

A few tears ran down her cheek after her story.

"Let me see the other collage—the one of our family," she said.

I handed her the family heirloom that glass had locked in time. Another smile washed across her face and another glimmer sparkled in her eyes. She reached up and caught a tear.

"You were the ugliest baby I've ever seen," she said with a hard laugh. "You looked like a chipmunk until you were four." More tears than she could catch streamed out, not from sadness, but from remembering. I just sat watching and listening.

"But you were so cute. Ugly babies grow up to be handsome men. That's what my mother always said." She moved on to the next picture. It was of me trying to hold Royal still and rinse the soap out of his hair. He looked like a wet rat.

"Royal," she said. "He hates getting a bath, doesn't he, Corey?"

"Yes Ma'am."

"But he's such a good dog."

Royal was lying beside my mother's chair, and she had a hand buried in his thick fur. His ears perked up when he heard his name.

"Whose dog is this?" I asked, pointing at the little puppy with her sister and brother.

"That was my first dog, Charlie. He had some kind of disease, and we had to put him to sleep. He couldn't walk anymore." She paused for a moment and thought about what she said.

"Kind of like me now, huh?" my mother said as she looked away from the collage and straight into my eyes with a penetrating stare, as if I could offer a way out.

At times her suffering seemed inhumane, an atrocity that I struggled to comprehend. And other times, it added some value to her life and to mine that had been absent. Sitting together, talking, laughing, and remembering, seemed to make this painful journey one worth embracing.

There was no doubt now that this horrible disease would take her life, but there was not going to be a quick shot in the shoulder blade to end her misery. She would see this one to the bitter end.

"This was taken at Sunset Beach. I was watching you

build a huge sand castle, and put your army men all around it." She started laughing again.

"We had to buy you new toys after every trip to the beach, because you always let the tide wash them away," she said, and let the collage rest on her legs.

"Corey, can we go back inside now. I'm tired."

Her strength was dwindling. She no longer had the relaxed look of comfort on her face, but a strained one, as if she were trying to hide the pain that was starting again. I carried her back to her room, set her down and tucked her into bed. I gave her a glass of water and a handful of pills. As I turned to leave, she grabbed my hand and said my name in such a way as to warrant my full and undivided attention.

"Yes Ma'am?"

"I love you son," she said softly, and put her head down on the pillow. I leaned down and kissed her forehead.

"I love you too, Mom," I said, and meant it with more heart than I ever knew I had.

Chapter 34

ROLY CARRIED THE TEAM through the fourth game of the playoffs. I sat in the dugout and kept the books, which was an easy task, as neither team had scored going into the seventh inning. There had been no hits and no errors committed in the field; baseball was executed flawlessly that night, and two no hitters were in progress. Every player on the field was eyes ahead, butts down, and all business. It was one of the quietest baseball games I've ever attended. There was no chatter from the players in the field or the dugouts, for fear it would break even their own concentration.

In the seventh inning, Roly was facing the top of Rockingham's line-up. The first hitter came to the plate and took his stance. He ended Roly's no-hitter with a shot down the third base line. A strikeout, an easy grounder, and we had two outs, with a runner on second base. When the Rockingham left fielder sent a fastball over the centerfield fence, I marked it in the book, and it didn't look good: two to nothing in the seventh inning.

The next batter grounded out to Godfrey at first, and the inning was over.

"Let's get those runs back. I wanna hear some bats cracking," Cavanaugh yelled, when the team came into the dugout.

There were no sounds of bats cracking on our side that inning. Their pitcher still had a no-hitter going into the eighth.

The next inning Roly got into trouble again and Cavanaugh brought Duffers to the mound to get us out of it, which he did. When the team entered the dugout, Cavanaugh was waiting for them.

"Do I need to remind you that whoever has more runs wins the game? If this is how you want it to end, then keep standing around looking at good pitches, and swinging at bad ones," Cavanaugh said, and walked out of the dugout.

The benches were silent. We had given up. Not a base hit all night, and now we needed several. Anything would do—just a walk, or an error in the field would help.

I read off the batting order, "Godfrey, Nichols, Tyler, and back to the top," I said.

Godfrey took his stance. The first pitch was a strike, and a real beaut, but Rod never swung at the first pitch, no matter what it looked like.

"Godfrey, that may have been the last strike you're ever gonna see boy. Get to work," Cavanaugh yelled, and clapped his hands together. He was fired up. He couldn't figure out what happened to his team.

Rod watched the next pitch, and argued with the umpire

when it was a called strike. Cavanaugh turned his back in disgust. He despised it when his ball players argued with the calls. There are a thousand decisions made in every ball game, and it was foolish to argue with just one. That's what he used to tell us. He said nothing to Rod, which was a bad sign. Rod struck out on the next pitch. Nichols and Tyler hit weak grounders and were thrown out easily. The Rockingham pitcher still had a no hitter going into the ninth inning.

Duffers closed Rockingham down, and the score was two to nothing, and it was our last bat—the last three outs. Unless we tied it up, there would be no more ball to play.

"Let's go you guys. Last three outs. It's now or never," Cole said.

Cavanaugh didn't say a word in the dugout. He didn't lecture us. He didn't give us a pep talk. He simply put in a wad of chewing tobacco and decided that it was our game to win or lose, in whatever manner we saw fit.

"Manny, Fitz, Miller, and Posie," I read off the order. We were at the top of our line-up. It was silent in our dugout. Coach Cavanaugh walked out to first base but gave no orders to Manny, who was at the plate.

The first pitch was high, but the second pitch was right down the center of the plate, and Todd got all of it. He broke the no-hitter with a double to left center. The Rockingham pitcher worked out of the stretch for the first time all night, with the tying run at the plate, and the fastest base runner in North Carolina on second base. Manny stole third base easily on the very next pitch, and the Rockingham coach came to the mound. He called all the infielders in, and they had a pow-wow.

I was nervous, and knew Fitz must have been too. He was at the plate. Cavanaugh gave a few signals, but none of them meant anything. Fitz was on his own. The pitcher moved the ball around the plate, not giving Fitz much to work with, and ended up walking him.

As Miller stepped up to the plate, everyone in our dug-out got up and stood along the fence. The tying run was on first, the go-ahead run at the plate, and no outs. One base hit and a walk in the ninth had turned things around. Fitz took a decisive lead at first, and the pitcher got nervous. He stepped off the mound, and Fitz stepped back to the bag. Fitz, seeing that he had the pitcher rattled, took a bigger lead the second time. The pitcher, against good judgment, tried to pick him off. He sent the ball over the first baseman's head and out of play. Manny scored from third, and Fitz took second base as a penalty. Two to one, and no outs. I noticed two Rockingham players move into the bullpen, as Miller stepped back into the batter's box. The Rockingham coach signaled to the pitcher to put him on first; giving them a force out at any base. With Miller on first and Fitz on second, and still no outs, things were looking good as Posie stepped up to the plate.

I watched Cavanaugh's signs and knew that he called for a hit and run. Posie took the signal and connected with the first pitch and sent a line drive right up the middle. Everyone was moving. The shot almost knocked the pitcher off his feet, but somehow he caught the ball. The place went crazy. Rockingham players were screaming at their pitcher to throw it to first. Our fans and players were yelling at Miller and Fitz to get back to their bases. Fitz stopped mid-stride and dove back to second base, but Miller didn't have a chance. The pitcher threw him out at first. How quickly things had turned around.

"Damnit," Miller yelled, and threw his batting helmet from first base to the dugout. It shattered and bounced around at our feet.

"Number sixteen. If I see that again you're out of here," the umpire yelled.

"Son, I don't even know what to say to you. Is that how you want me to remember you?" Cavanaugh said from first base.

With two outs, down two to one in the bottom of the ninth, we had only one glimmer of hope: Fitz was in scoring position on second base.

"Good eye, good eye, pick the one you want," Cavanaugh said to Jackson, who was in the batter's box.

He sent a shot down the first base line. He couldn't have picked a better spot to hit it. Fitz was moving; he rounded third with no signs of letting up. It was all or nothing now. The right fielder played the ball perfectly, and swiftly made a throw to the plate. The catcher called out to let the throw come though, meaning no cutoff. The second baseman moved aside and watched as we all did, with apprehension. The ball skipped off the mound, perfectly on target. The catcher had the plate blocked and was waiting on the ball.

"Hit the dirt," Cavanaugh yelled, but Fitz either didn't hear him, or decided against it. The ball reached the plate at the same moment Seth collided with the Rockingham catcher. The umpire took the scene in, and yelled, "You're out!"

There were yells and screams coming from every direction. Cavanaugh was running towards home plate, the other umpire, who stood near second base was yelling and pointing at something. Fitz and the downed Rockingham catcher were slow to get to their feet, but when they did, the umpire noticed the ball was lying in the dirt, not in the catcher's mitt.

"Safe!" the umpire corrected his call.

The Rockingham coach started to dispute the call, but when he saw his catcher lean down and pick up the baseball, the coach knew that the call had been fair. Fitz's decision to go in standing up had tied up the ball game.

Two outs, tied 2 to 2 in the ninth inning, with Jackson in scoring position on second, Frank Roystone stepped up to the plate. The Rockingham coach came onto the field, followed by a relief pitcher, and pulled the starting pitcher who had given up only 2 base hits, both of them in the ninth inning. We all waited as the new guy warmed up.

Stoney was what coach Cavanaugh called his secret weapon. He was one of the best hitters on the team, but he batted in the seventh spot. A pitcher learns that the good hitters are usually at the top of the line-up, so Cavanaugh put Stoney at the bottom, to add a little weight to our string. The new pitcher was left handed, and so was Frank.

The first pitch was perfect, right down the middle of the plate, and not much movement on the ball. I was glad to see that their relief pitcher was nothing like Duffers. Had he been, it would have remained a tie ball game. Stoney had a smile on his face when he stepped into the box for the second pitch. He got every last stitch of the ball, and sent it to the fence. Jackson scored easily from second base, and the Hillcrest Bulldogs were going to the State Championship.

Chapter 35

AFTER THE GAME I WENT STRAIGHT HOME. My father was sitting in the dark when I entered the living room. Only a scarce amount of light from a street lamp lit the room. I noticed my father's eyes were glistening, and it was the first time I could ever recall him not commenting about a ball game. He said nothing.

"What's wrong, Dad?" I asked.

"We need to talk about what we are going to do."

When he turned his face towards mine, I saw tears streaming down his cheek. The Giant did in fact have tears, I thought to myself. He has glands to produce them, and ducts to carry them.

"What we are going to do about what, Dad?" I asked.

"Your mother, Corey. She is getting much worse. The doctors think she would be better off in the hospital."

"No. No way," I answered, emphatically. "I made her a promise, and I am going to keep it, no matter how bad it gets."

"Corey, I don't think you understand just how bad it is going to be."

"I don't care, Dad. She would do the same for us. We have come this far. How can we quit now and walk away? They'll put her on a respirator in the hospital and keep her alive when she should die... No way," I said, and left the room.

I found my mother sleeping when I reached the end of the hall. Beside her was Bob Marley's biography lying face up open to the last photograph taken of him. The caption read, "BadWeisse Cancer Clinic, Germany." The always-smiling Bob Marley looked morose.

I laid down beside her and found her hand. I wondered how she could be so sick when she is awake, to look so peaceful when she is asleep. I wished I could have at least said good night.

I moved my fingers around her skin, the way she had been doing with mine. Her veins were prominent, and her skin was soft and warm. I wished she would just stay asleep now and dream for the rest of her life. I laid there and watched the ceiling fan go around and around. The shadows were moving much slower than the blades. I heard Royal in the bushes just outside the window. He ruffled some leaves looking for his spot. When he found it, he let out a long, deep howl and plopped down. It woke my mother.

"Corey?" she said.

"Yes Ma'am. I'm here."

We laid there in silence for a long time, but I knew she was awake. Her breathing was strained, not peaceful and quiet like it was when she was asleep.

"Corey, I can not think so good," she said. "Different than the medicine. My tongue feels heavy, and I can't move my eyes."

I held her hand tightly, hoping it would make her feel a little better to know she was not alone.

"Thinking about dying and knowing that it is coming soon, it makes me feel better to remember when I was a child. I saw things differently back then; maybe better than I see them now. Children don't know what death is. They don't want absolute answers. They just want to dream."

"I don't know what I'm going to do when you die, mom. It's just not fair."

When she didn't say anything for a long time, I felt ashamed for saying what I had. I pitied myself when my mother was the one dying.

"I guess I'm being selfish," I continued. "Whatever I have to deal with is half of what you are going through."

"I don't think so, Corey. I am going to a better place, and I am not scared anymore. I am only worried about you."

"I don't believe in that. What if there is nothing else? What if this is it?"

"That's a thought I can't bare to think. I only have two things keeping my chin up: you and something better waiting for me when I die. I can't expect you to understand that, but when your day comes I'll bet you will."

She turned her head slightly and looked at me. "I'll bet you will," she said again.

"Maybe so, Mom. I'll cross that bridge when I get to it—same as you."

"Corey, will you give me my medicine, please?"

I went to the bathroom and got a handful of pills and

handed them to her with a glass of water. I lay down beside her, and in silence, we both pondered what life would hold for us when this nightmare was over.

"Mom, do you remember your wish the night on the baseball field?"

"Of course I do."

"Well, it has come true. Our days of fighting are forgotten in my mind. I remember nothing but the good things about you: how beautiful you are; how strong you are, how much courage you have, and how much you have taught me in just two months. That is what I will remember forever. And I am going to think of you when I see the world, through two sets of eyes—mine and yours."

"Thank you, Corey," my mother said, and squeezed my hand.

I kissed her on the forehead and felt tears welling up inside of me, but I did not want her to see them. Our roles needed to change. I needed her strength and she needed my adolescence.

The pain medicine slowed her breathing until it was rhythmic and peaceful again, and she was asleep.

That night I drove to Raven's Rock to watch the sunrise. Royal and I sat together on a rock in the middle of the river. He heard every critter scampering in the woods, and I heard nothing. Once again, I thought about the beauty of being a canine. He has no idea what is going on, I thought. I wondered why the doctors did not find the cancer earlier, when they could have treated it. I wondered if my mother would have gotten cancer if we had stayed in Virginia;

had we not moved to North Carolina. I needed someone or something to blame, but I came up short. There was a time when I wanted to run from this place, from this life of mine, because of how much I hated my mother, and how miserable she made my life, and now, I want to run from this place because of how much I love her.

'Sixteen miles downstream from the birthplace of George Washington, where the Shenandoah River comes out of the Blue Ridge Mountains carrying sycamore leaves and acorns.' I remembered my mother's words about where she was from, and where I was born. I thought about the farm, and the life we had once had, and how quickly things had changed, how different they had become. That quiet, beautiful place in the Shenandoah Mountains is where Linda Wails was from, and in the sand hills of North Carolina is where she will die.

When the sun rose out of the river, I realized I had not moved in six hours. The sky was crimson and gold, and the Cape Fear River cut a wide path through the heart of North Carolina.

Chapter 36

THE AIR WAS ACRID, PUNGENT AND CHOKING. I stood at the end of a hallway—long and narrow. I heard a voice and listened more intently, more carefully. Banging, banging, banging in my chest. I thought it would explode. I took a deep breath. It was worse than I thought. The air was not pungent; it was putrid from blood, flesh, and bone. I counted the paces … seventeen, seventeen long steps to the end of the hall.

The walls were black and the light uneven. Life was moving in and out of the shadows of a swinging halogen lamp. Overhead, it passed back and forth, back and forth, like the pendulum of a Grandfather clock, but there was no ticking, only the breeze on my skin as it passed. The sound of hacksaws gnawing at a thing was ringing in my ears, so I covered them, and wished I had three more hands: two for my eyes, and one for my nose.

Eyes were staring from the walls, beady, yellow eyes, slit like a cat's, and obsidian like a vulture's; hiding in the shadows, lurking in the blackness; the place where lives are altered forever.

A deep, achy moan penetrated my ears. It entered between the cracks in my fingers, and went straight for my heart; soothing for a second, massaging gently, and when I was relaxed, it cut deep into the soft tissue, and I clutched at my chest.

"Breathe, Corey," a soft whisper, serpentine, and seductive, came from the walls. "Take a deep breath," the voice said.

The lamp swung away. I stood in the shadows, and a fat man smoking a cigarette stood in the light. He was smiling, and then he was gone. I felt my pupils growing and the heat of the lamp on my skin as it swung back. The fat man took a pull from his cigarette, lazily. A long tail of embers fell from its tip. I watched them roll off and fall to the ground, and heard the sizzle when they landed. Blood was coursing into a drain on the floor, smeared all over the man's face, and on his hands. He thumped the cigarette away, and grabbed a saw. The teeth were silver, and shiny. I was looking so hard the light burnt my eyes. I heard the saw gnawing—chkt, chkt, chk, the sharp teeth scratching, clawing, and cutting. I wrapped my arms around myself and stood scared—scared of what I would see when the light swung back.

"They're almost done, Corey. I'll be ready to go soon," a sweet voice called out in the dark.

I awoke to screaming. They were ringing in my ears, and echoing through the house. A door slammed open and hit the back of the wall. My father was running down the long corridor leading to the back bedroom. I sat up and looked at my mother. She was sitting bolt upright in the bed, screaming like an opera singer. Sweat was pouring from her forehead. What hair was left on her scalp was soaked and matted. Her eyes were closed, but her mouth was wide open and her yells were deafening. I could not move. I just sat there watching.

"Linda ... Linda," my father yelled over her screams. He shook her easily. "You were having a nightmare, that's all. It's over now, honey," my father said consolingly.

"They were cutting them off, Robert," she said in a panic.

"Cutting what off, Linda?" he asked.

"My legs," she said, as if he had asked a dumb question.

"Do you want some more medicine?"

"No."

My father braced her narrow shoulders in his hands. Her eyes were wide open and deep in their sockets. Her beautiful face was distorted with pain. The cancer and the large doses of medication that were making her sickness barely endurable were taking their toll. Her shoulders were frail; her blouse hung low in the front; her collar bone could be traced the entire distance of her chest. Her frailty did not exude beauty the way a photographer accents the slender clavicle of a model. It looked more like the clavicle of a mannequin; a lifeless reconstruct used to teach anatomy. Dark circles surrounded her eyes, and her lips were scaly and cracking; the price of so many pain pills and syrups.

"I need to go to the bathroom, will you bring it to me?" she said.

She licked her lips, ran her tongue across her gums, and sucked her cheeks together, searching for enough saliva to swallow. Her hair was thin, so bare in places her scalp was visible. She could reach up and pull out a handful of the wiry dead strands, barely rooted. Her thoughts were cluttered; her mind no longer able to make the normal associations it once had. It was as difficult to think as it was to breathe or to swallow.

"I can take you to the bathroom, Linda. Is that what you want?" my father replied, like a man trying to teach his children the proper association of words: the difference between "take" and "bring."

A wrinkle across my mother's forehead signaled that her synapses fired properly and she realized her blunder. A smile crossed her face as she thought about how ridiculous it was to ask my father to bring her the bathroom, as if it were a glass of water; but she wished it were that easy as she began the arduous task of getting herself there.

She leaned back on one arm, and struggled to work her legs free of the blankets. My father gently placed his hand beneath her knees, and helped her to swing around. She looked down at her legs with a grimace on her face as if she were staring at someone else's appendages. She curled her toes into the shag carpet, making sure it was her feet she would be standing on. Her hand sunk into the mattress and she tried to push herself up. Her first attempt to stand failed. Her chest rose with the effort of getting another breath; she moved her tongue across her chapped lips, and then inside her mouth to feel her gums. She found another morsel of saliva for one more swallow.

She was dying. I watched a woman whose single greatest quality had been strength, struggle with the simplest tasks that we all perform every second of every day.

The lines of her gaunt face strengthened, her lips

creased, and she pushed as hard as she could. Her body came off the bed and her legs wobbled under the strain; the silk pajamas, draped over her bony knees, unfurled to the floor. She was shaky, confused, and unstable; so frail and so delicate. My father bent down and steadied her at the hips. She realigned herself, adjusted her weight, and stood tall. She thanked my father and took a step towards the bathroom.

Chapter 37

WITHOUT THE AID OF RADIATION TREATMENT and chemotherapy, my mother's plight grew worse by the hour. The cancer spread from her lymph nodes to her blood cells, to her bone marrow, and eventually to all of her organs, and finally her brain. Her nightmares grew worse and much more frequent. At first they only occurred at night, but as time went on they moved to day time as well—just about anytime she was asleep they snuck in and haunted her. We talked about them and it's not something I care to remember. Her pain was of a grandeur that few of us will ever experience in our lives. She cried out in the night with screams that woke me and had me running down the hallway to her side. I tried to talk to her, but she usually remained locked in the darkness: the horror that was running rampant through her mind.

I grew tired watching her suffer, and daily my father and I refused hospital administrators the right to take her from our home. I made a promise to her, and I was going to keep it. She was not going to spend one single day in the hospital. It was a family matter now. She would be cared for at home, she would suffer at home, and she would die at home. There would be no other way.

I continued to carry her to the bathroom when she had the strength to get cleaned up, and eventually my father and I had to perform the chore while she lie in bed. She talked in crazy, inaudible languages, and every now and then would form words, but not in logical order. Her mind was bleeding, like wet ink on paper.

The brain cancer came fast and with reckless abandon. It clouded her thoughts completely, and delivered a decisive blow to my morale. She no longer knew who I was.

I was scared to walk down her hallway, and into her room. It was a place I never wanted to visit again. I stopped holding her hand, and I stopped dreaming her dreams. I was scared of the disease in her mind, and was worried that it would attack mine.

The sand, set in motion forty-five days ago, was running faster. One hourglass chamber was almost empty, and a new one almost full.

"Ooooooooh, Ooooooooooh," I heard the moans coming from her room, and hurried to get down the hallway. When I reached her, I noticed her eyes were open, but not focusing on anything. She was yelling, and it was deafening. It seemed like her vocal chords were the only thing left intact. They could still carry a tune and hold a pitch as loud as an opera singer for minutes on end.

I quickly filled a syringe with the purple syrup that was her only savior now. I reached out with my left hand and got a firm grip on her jaw. My fingers sunk in around her face, as she tried to swivel her head and bare her teeth to bite me. When I had her mouth opened and her strength to fight subsided, I shot the thick purple fluid down her throat. She gargled and spit out what she could, but most of the stream made it into her mouth. Her screaming faded within a minute, and I felt the muscles in her face relax. The medication I was giving her was used only for people as sick as her, dying a painful death. As the pain eased, she slumped back into the bed. Her physical body floated away and her mental existence took over. She was concentrating on breathing. Up and down, up and down, her chest was moving to the rhythm of the air entering and leaving her lungs.

Her eyes fixed on me. A hand waved in mid air, closing several times as if she had caught something. I put my hand in her path and she made contact. She felt my hand for several seconds; her bony fingers ran over my skin.

"Corey? Is that you?"

She had not said my name in weeks. It was heartbreaking to think she did not know who I was any longer. And for some reason, I wanted more than anything in the world for her to know that is was me still taking care of her, and would be until the end.

"Yes Ma'am. It's me, mom," I said.

"Corey, will you cut them off, please?" she asked in a sweet voice.

"Cut what off?"

"My legs."

I just stood there hoping the thought would pass, and quickly. I didn't understand her detachment.

She took a deep breath; her tongue extended over her

bottom lip, and the purple pain syrup ran down her chin.

"Corey, will you sit with me?"

"Of course," I answered.

I was scared. Just the sight of her scared me now. I did not know what death actually looked like, until that night when it reached out and put a cold finger on my heart. The touch left me numb. Linda Wails was staring down a dark alley, and did not want to walk it alone.

I felt my paleness, but saw it in her skin. I wanted to turn on every light in the house, thinking that would make it better. I wanted to run to the bathroom and be sick. I just wanted out. I wanted her to die. I wanted it to be over. Edgar Allen Poe could not have concocted a more horrific picture than the one before my eyes: my mother's gaunt face, swollen lips and tongue, and the thick purple residue covering her teeth. I fought through it. I had to. She knew who I was again, for the last time in her life, and I knew she would not live much longer.

I switched on a lamp next to her bed, and the light made it better. She did not look so much like a ghost lingering in the dark. She took another deep breath, and used the air to tell me she was dying. Her eyes were fixed on the ceiling.

"I know, Mom," I said, with tears running down my face.

"I always wanted to see the Sahara Desert. Have you ever seen it?" she asked.

By now I was used to her ludicrous questions; the brain cancer and drugs making her say crazy things. Of course, I had not seen the Sahara Desert.

"I've seen pictures," I strained a reply. The Sahara Desert was the furthest thing from my mind, and I wondered why it was on hers.

"Not the same. I'll bet it's beautiful," she replied.

She could not move a muscle. The strong pain medicine I administered with the syringe had paralyzed her. Her body was rigid, eyes ahead, looking straight at the ceiling. Her breathing was rhythmic, strained, and slow.

"Corey, what do you think Heaven is like?" she asked.

I did not answer. I could not speak.

"Do you think it is a glass city like the Bible says?" she asked.

"I don't know, Mom."

"Give me your hand," she said.

I placed my hand in hers, but she did not squeeze back and her fingers did not caress my skin; the feeling she had grown so fond of.

"Do you think I can play cards with my father in Heaven?" she asked.

"Maybe you can do whatever you want in Heaven."

"Are you going to be okay, son?"

"Yes Ma'am."

The pain medicine soon did its job, and she was asleep. I laid beside her, holding her hand, and dreamed her dreams for the last time:

There is nothing here. Light spreads out evenly across a million grains of sand. There are no hills to block the view, and no forests to splinter the light. There are no shadows to hide behind in this place. In the absence of everything is the purest of beauty.

Blue and translucent, the sky spreads out. Deep orange,

and rising, the sun is a thousand Earthly mountains.

A child stands wide-eyed in front of it all—a little girl. And a man stands in the distance, waiting for her to come to him. She sees him, and starts to run. Her feet hardly touch the ground, weightless, and effortlessly, she crosses the desert.

The man is dressed sharply; an olive fedora on his head and gold locks poking out underneath; a white shirt, khaki pants, and well-oiled boots on his feet. The Time Keeper stands stoic looking at a pocket watch.

"I have been waiting on you," he says.

He picks her up, hugs her, and nibbles on her ear. "Stop it, Daddy," the girl says, and laughs at her father.

"I have a lot to show you," he says, and sets her down. They hold hands and begin their walk.

"Look, Daddy, the sky is full of butterflies."

There was a butterfly for every grain of sand in the desert; colors indescribable on Earth. The sky was full of God's gift to dreamers.

"I never knew you liked butterflies so much," the man says, glancing to the sky.

"Did I do that?" the little girl says.

"Yes. They came with you."

When I woke up, I was alone. Linda Wails died in her sleep, but she knew I was there holding her hand right to the end. 'It is the natural way of things, Corey, for children to carry the burden of their parent's death,' my mother had said to me, and I remembered those words as I kissed her forehead and closed her eyes. 'This is a burden we all share.'

I went to the living room and startled my father when I woke him.

"What? What is it?" He said, jumping out of the chair.

"Dad," I said, but could say no more. I squeezed him as hard as I could and cried.

"What Corey? What?" he said in an erratic voice.

He loosened my grip and ran back to my mother's room. He switched on every light in the house on his way, but that wasn't going to bring her back. He called 911 and the emergency crews were there in five minutes. I sat in the recliner while they wheeled machine after machine into the house. After what seemed like eternity, I got up and made my way through the crew in the hallway and into my mother's room. They had needles in her arms, IV's running, a heart monitor attached, and electric shocking devices laid out all over the bed and the room.

"Are you crazy! She's dead. Let her die. She has suffered enough!" I was screaming. I pushed one of the men away from her.

"Get out of here!" I yelled.

My father wrapped me up in his arms and held me still, trying to calm me down.

"What are they doing, Dad?" I yelled and tried to get free. "Tell them to get out of here. NOW!"

My dad was silent. His body was trembling, same as mine. The nightmare was finally over.

Chapter 38

On THE SECOND DAY OF JUNE, Linda Wails was pronounced dead at six thirty in the morning, as if we needed a crew of paramedics to tell us. On that day I lost sight of who was controlling things in this world. Why should a force greater than ourselves torture my mother and me with disgust, to wipe the slate clean, and torture us with endearment that would not last? At seventeen years old my life lay in a shattered pile of broken glass. The pieces had been delicately held together by the sinew of compassion I felt for my mother, and now reflected the image of a confused boy. It just couldn't be ... how could so many things end on the same day? Tonight was the night of the state championship; the night I would play my last baseball game with the best friends I would ever know. College scholarships had come to fruition, prospects of playing in the pros were dawning, but it didn't seem to matter anymore.

Our house was full of people: people from the church, family, friends, funeral coordinators, co-workers of my parents, and teachers from my school. Everything and everyone made me angry just to look at it: the flowers people were sending, the cards with their sentiments, the minister talking in tongues, and the funeral coordinators talking about how beautiful the ceremony would be. Where were they in the middle of the nights when my father and I were taking care of her? Where were they when she was screaming in pain? They had no right to be in my house. They had no right to say prayers for her or plan her funeral. She would not have wanted any of it. She made peace with everything she had a conflict with and it was over. Why couldn't these people just leave us alone?

As I sat alone in my room, with my fists clenched, I realized how tightly I was holding on to the idea of fairness. Was it fair that I was robbed of my mother while we were both so young? It was this idea, this notion of mine, this self pity I was prone to, that my mother had tried to cure. If I was ever going to make it I had to let it go.

I thought about all the trips we made to the cemetery where her father was buried. I let my mind take me back and I watched her get out of the car and walk to her father's grave carrying an arrangement of red and white roses. She would stand over his grave and just stare. She would look at the ground where he lay, and eventually tears would stream from her eyes. Were her tears because she missed him? Was she crying because she remembered him so vividly that it seemed real? I thought about myself in her shoes. I will visit her grave. I will stand over it and talk to it. I will remember her strength, and wish she could see her creation as I grow and accomplish things. I will look at her headstone and see the letters of my mother's name, Linda Wails, written in fancy, swirled letters.

While engraving in my mind the lessons I had learned from my mother in her last days on Earth, I felt something indescribable, as if some vital thing inside of me, like the cogs of a clock, had finally stopped grinding against one another.

I need to make sure that her efforts do not go in vain, I thought to myself. I need to put our talks to good use. I need to make her proud of me. For her, I have something to live for and something to achieve, but what I do not know.

I could hear the people milling around in the house; vaguely I could hear their voices. I could hear them in the halls, in the living room, in the bathroom, all the rooms except my mother's. No one dared to venture down that long dark hallway. I wondered what was still there and what had been taken away? That thought was the first tangible one I had all day; the first thought that could be measured.

Were her clothes still there? Were all the bottles of pills and syrups still there? Was the syringe still lying on the table? The metal chair with rubber stoppers on the legs —was it still in the shower? The electric wheel chair that she flat out refused to use, was it still sitting in the corner of the room? The wrap she wore on her head, the velvet, burgundy wrap that she always wore to cover her bald head, was it lying in the bed? The book I had given her, "Catch a Fire," the book about Bob Marley's life, was it still on the bed side table with her Bible? How long will her things stay there? Who will get rid of them and what will they do with them? Box them up and put them in the attic, throw them away, sell them? How long will that room remain the hourglass chamber that my mother lived in for 2 months? How long?

I heard a knock on my door, not a loud booming knock, but a soft tapping, as if someone wanted to come in, but they didn't want to try too hard. Again, I heard the tapping.

"Who is it?" I asked.

"It's Emily, Corey."

Slowly, I got up from the bed and opened the door. Emily's eyes were red, swollen, and puffy, and she looked so sad. I wondered about that. Why today? Why today are things any different? Why should she be crying so hard today? Today is the greatest release Linda Wails has ever experienced, I thought. She is free. Her suffering has finally ended. I then had my second clear thought of the day: Emily isn't crying for my mother, she's crying about what is left behind.

"Corey, I'm so ..." Emily started.

"Em, you don't have to say anything," I said. "Come sit down with me."

Emily sat down on the edge of my bed and I sat next to her.

"You know what ...," I said. "My mother said my name again last night. Just before she died, she said, 'Corey, is that you?' ... and she asked me if I was going to be okay. Can you believe that? I can't remember the last time she knew who anyone was?"

Emily didn't say anything. She wiped some more tears from her cheek.

"Tell me why you're crying, Emily."

"What do you mean, Corey? It just doesn't seem fair," Emily said.

"I don't know about it being fair or not, that's not for us to decide, but I do understand this is the way things are. We couldn't change it, but we did make the most of it. Didn't we?"

"You did," Emily said.

I felt a strength inside of me that I had never known. Perhaps my mother had given me all she had left before leaving this world.

"It really doesn't have to be so sad, Emily. My mother wasn't sad. I don't see why we should be. I've heard about the crazy thing of celebrating someone's life when they die, but I've never really had a reason to think about it. It's making sense today," I said.

Emily looked at me dumbfounded, and I noticed how uneasy she was, wondering what to say, or worried she may say the wrong thing.

"My mother kept saying she would have liked two years back to live differently. When I'm dying I hope I don't want to ask for any back, not a minute to do something I left undone," I said. "But you know what I have been wondering about the most today?"

"What, Corey?"

"I wonder how my mother found so much peace at the end of her life? I know I changed a lot too, and that had something to do with it, but that wasn't all of it. She was calmer than I ever remembered her. She became so gentle after she got sick. That wasn't like her, not even when I was growing up, before her first bout with cancer. Something about dying made a radical change in her. I know you don't know the answer. I doubt if anyone can answer that question, but I wonder what it is, what is it that makes a person change when they know their life will be over soon, and why do we wait until the end to change?"

"I don't know, Corey," Emily said in earnest.

"If anything about this isn't fair, that would be it. It's not fair that we all live telling ourselves that tomorrow we'll change. Only tomorrow we're worse off than we are today. My mother did it for almost twenty years. She told me so. Every day she said she was going to make a change and she never did."

"What did she want to change?" Emily asked.

"Just little things, like going places, getting a degree from college, being a better mother and a better wife. That's what she said anyway."

"And what about you?"

"That's the question isn't it? That was the question before any of this with my mother started, and it's still the question now. What do I want to do?"

"Corey, I didn't mean it that way," Emily said quickly. "Please don't think I meant …"

"It's okay, Emily," I said. "I know what you meant."

I knew how uncomfortable Emily was. I could see it in her face. She had probably stood outside my door for an hour wondering what words she would say to me, and asking me today, of all days, about my intentions were certainly not among them.

"I know you didn't mean it that way, but if anyone has a right to know what I am thinking it's you," I continued. "I am fine, Em. You have to believe me when I tell you that. My mother said it was her job to see that I would be all right when this was over. She didn't fail at her last task. I have already cried all I intend to, I have said my good-byes, and I have no regrets, not now. My mother died holding my hand, we—"

I burst into tears.

"Corey, it's all right to cry. You can't hold it all in," she said.

"We couldn't have asked for anything more. Could we?" I finished.

"No, you couldn't," Emily said.

I pulled myself together quickly, dried my eyes, and continued:

"I don't know where that came from, man," I said, and cleared my throat.

Emily's face was helpless, as she put her arms around me and hugged me tightly.

"Whatever's on your mind, Corey … I'll listen and I'll try to understand. I promise. And whatever you need to do, I'll wait for you."

Emily's words were intuitive. It was this thing about Emily Vallent that I could never understand—her knack of discovering the unspoken. Emily's calming words put my heart to rest, and I realized I was not all alone in the world like I had once feared.

A moment later, I heard Cole's voice coming from the living room.

"What time is it?" I asked urgently.

"I don't know. It's about 6 o'clock I think," Emily replied.

I jumped up from the bed and started getting my things together for the game.

"You're not going to the game, are you?" Emily asked in disbelief.

"Are you kidding me? There isn't a thing in this world that could keep me from this game."

I kissed Emily on the cheek and headed out to the living room. At the doorway, I looked back, and thanked Emily for her words.

The living room was packed; Cole and my father were talking in the kitchen. Cole was dressed out in his uniform and ready to go. When he saw me coming across the living room with my gear, he had the same look Emily had, disbelief.

"Don't look so surprised, Cole. You didn't really think I would miss this game, did you?"

Cole made no reply.

"Good luck," my father said, and shook Cole's hand. He turned to me, wrapped me up in his massive arms, and spoke for only me to hear: "I'm proud of you, son," he said. "Play with your heart tonight."

"I intend to," I replied.

Chapter 39

CAVANAUGH was standing in the parking lot making sure the bus was loaded and everyone was onboard. He was talking to the assistant coach when Cole and I pulled up. Cavanaugh showed no surprise that I was there. The game is what I had always lived for; he knew I would be there.

"On the double, gentlemen," Cavanaugh said. "This bus is leaving in 5 minutes."

Cole and I grabbed our gear and loaded up. The bus ride was so quiet that when Jackson pulled out a tin of tobacco and packed it down firm, the thump, thump on the lid sounded like a bass drum inside the bus. Other than our breathing, it was the only sound for the entire ride.

As soon as the bus came to a stop, everyone rose quickly and started getting off.

"Sit back down," Cavanaugh said. "I have a few words for you before we take the field."

There was some commotion as everyone got back into

their seats. The driver closed the doors, and quickly it became as quiet as the ride there had been. Cavanaugh stood at the front of the bus eyeing his team. He stared at each of us for a long while before saying anything.

"Manny, why are we here tonight?" he finally said.

"To win, Coach," Manny replied. He was the only one on the bus with a grin on his face. Sometimes I thought his face was fixed that way permanently, and I wondered what could ever be so pressing on Todd Manny to wipe away his smile.

"Fitz, why are we here?" Cavanaugh said.

"Because we've earned it," Fitz replied.

"O'Conner?"

"Because we've beaten everyone else," Cole said, and the mood slackened. "This is the state championship, Coach. Didn't anyone tell you?"

"Wails. Why are we here tonight?" Cavanaugh said, ignoring Cole's question.

"To play baseball," I replied.

"Stoney, why are we here?"

"To win it all."

Cavanaugh went from player to player asking only that one question: why are we here? In the end, after hearing him repeat it so many times, I wondered if Cavanaugh was even talking about baseball.

"Well gentleman, all things come to an end sooner or later, for us that day is today. Let's get all we can out of what's left," Cavanaugh said.

"Manny, you're leading off in center. Fitz, you're hitting second at short. Miller, third, at second base. Posie, you're hitting clean-up, behind the plate …"

"Stoney, you're hitting seventh tonight at third base. Godfrey, eighth, at first. Wails, you're on the mound, batting ninth."

Cavanaugh removed the game ball from its small brown, box. He rubbed it in his hands for a few seconds, really squeezing and pressing it into his palms to wear off the coating of newness. "Make everything count tonight," Cavanaugh said, and tossed me the game ball. Those were the words we took to the field for the North Carolina State Championship.

"Ladies and Gentlemen, please stand for the singing of the National Anthem," crackled through the speakers. I looked down the first base line at all my teammates; Cavanaugh stood closest to the plate. I was amazed that while the rest of us had a sullen, almost worried look, Cavanaugh's expression had not changed. He looked like he did on any other game night. It could have been the first game of the season or the last of the glory days. Cavanaugh's face gave away nothing.

It took me a lot of years, but I understood Cavanaugh clearly that night. He was not proud of us because of where we stood, but how we stood there. We had earned the right to stand in this line-up; a right that no one could ever take away. We stood as a team, no one player better than the next; and we stood nothing like the ballplayers we used to be, nothing like the kids we were years ago. Cavanaugh had changed all of that.

When the last note ricocheted off the rafters, we donned our caps and took the field. It's just another game of baseball, I kept trying to tell myself; it's just like any other game.

I was remiss of the world around me. I watched it fade into oblivion and funnel into the center of a catcher's mitt. Mike dropped three fingers down, calling for a slider. I stepped off the mound, confused. He stood up, stripped off his mask, and yelled, "Just makin' sure you're with me, Wails," punched his glove, and got back into position.

I threw a fastball as hard as I could. Mike shook his hand where it stung him and the umpire yelled, "Steee-rike One!"

Now we could play ball.

Miller kicked up some dirt and rubbed his hands in the clay. Stoney popped his glove with his bare hand and started some chatter.

"Go after him, Corey," Seth said.

I wasted a pitch high and tight. The batter swung and missed; a curve—he missed again; a fastball right down the pike—and the first strike-out of the State Championship. Mike sent the ball down to Stoney at third, and it moved like a blur across the infield, from player to player, and back to me. We retired the side easily that first inning, and a baseball had never felt so small in my hand.

"I want to hear some bats crackin'," Cavanaugh said, put in a wad of chew, and took his post at first base. Jim read off the batting line-up, just because we always did. "Manny, Fitz, Miller, and Posie," he said.

Cavanaugh signaled for a bunt—first pitch, first batter. Manny laid it down perfectly and stood on first base in four seconds flat.

"Pick a good one, Fitz," Cavanaugh yelled.

Seth took his stance and rapped the second pitch into center. The stands went wild, and everyone was on their feet in the dugout. Miller stepped into the batter's box. He watched the first pitch, got his bearings, and stepped into the box for the second. He sent a shot up the middle. Manny scored easily and Fitz was on third. The Charlotte coach came to the mound, took the game ball from his starting pitcher, and called for another. The pitcher walked off the field with his head hung low and his cap pulled down over his eyes. We were three for three, with a double, two singles, one run scored, and no outs in the first inning.

The new pitcher faired much better, shutting down Posie, Nichols, and Parker, and the score remained one to nothing until the sixth inning.

I walked the first hitter in the sixth and their third baseman sent a fastball over the centerfield fence. We were down a run going into the seventh. When I came into the dugout Cavanaugh was waiting for me.

"You know better than that, son. If you keep throwing it down the pike to that kid, you're gonna be collecting balls in the road all night," Cavanaugh said. "Use your head."

Charlotte kept us off the bases in the seventh, thanks to a lucky diving catch by their left fielder, robbing Stoney of a double. Charlotte started the next inning with two solid line drives, and I had men on first and second. I was worried. Either my fastball had lost its movement, or they were learning how to hit it, and my curve wasn't dropping off like it should.

Cavanaugh came to the mound. He took the game ball from my glove, and I stood there watching him turn it over and over in his hand, hoping he would give it back.

"What's the problem, son?" Cavanaugh said.

"There's no problem, Coach," I replied. I couldn't stop

staring at the game ball, wondering if Cavanaugh would give it back. "I'll get out of this," I said.

"If your curve isn't working, then don't throw it," Cavanaugh snapped. "Move the ball around the plate. Use the corners. That's what they're there for." Cavanaugh put the ball back in my glove. "Bear down," he said, and walked off the mound.

Fitz and Miller started some chatter as I stepped onto the mound. Every inning it was the same thing: I had men on base all night, and was forced to pitch out of the stretch causing my legs to tire.

I noticed the runner on second had a big lead. His legs were bent, spring loaded, and he was ready to go. I glanced up at Fitz. He gave me the signal for a pick-off. I looked back at the plate, held my stance for an instant, spun around to my left, and let the ball go. The runner was caught off-guard, and didn't stand a chance of getting back to the bag. He broke towards third, and Fitz and Stoney caught him in a run down and tagged him out.

"Way to look alive out there," Cavanaugh yelled.

I needed all the help I could get, and was using it. I turned my attention back to the hitter, giving him not much to work with on the next two pitches. He waited, forcing me to give him something in the strike zone. He sent a shot up the middle. Fitz made a diving stab, flipped the ball to Miller, and they turned a double play to end the inning.

The score remained two to one, Charlotte's lead, going into the eighth.

Chapter 40

"**B**OTTOM OF THE LINE-UP," Roly announced. "Stoney, Godfrey, Wails, and back to Manny."

Stoney and Godfrey both hit weak grounders and were thrown out easily. When my turn at the plate came, I was scared to swing for fear of missing the ball, so I just crowded the plate hoping for either a walk or to get hit; whatever it took to get on base. I ended up with a walk. As I tossed my bat towards the dugout and started down the line, I heard the Charlotte coach coming onto the field.

"Johnny!" he yelled. "That's gonna cost us big. Come on now. This is no time to let up."

Several girls stood up in the bleachers, and in unison they yelled out Manny's name. He shot them a wide grin, tucked his gold chain into his jersey, and got down to business. He knocked the dirt off his cleats and stepped into the box.

He connected on the third pitch for a solid single to left center. I stood on second base wishing that somehow

Manny and I could trade places. With me in front of him, I was doing nothing but standing in his way. He could have stolen third easily, and been that much closer to tying this game up. I didn't wish for very long, because on the very next pitch, with Fitz in the batter's box, the pitcher threw a wild pitch that sailed over the catcher's head and hit the backstop. Manny and I both advanced a base.

With two outs, down a run in the eighth inning, Charlotte was trying their best to lose the game; a walk and a passed ball had put them in a bad spot, and us in the driver's seat. Their coach called for a time-out and had a meeting on the mound with all the infielders. He whined like a little leaguer, and I could hear some of his words from where I stood on third base. He asked his team what the hell they were trying to do, give the game away? Those were my thoughts exactly.

Fitz took his stance. The stadium was quiet. There was no chatter from the Charlotte dugout or ours. I could hear my cleats in the clay as I took my lead.

"Pick a good one," Cavanaugh said and slapped his hands together. "Gotta have it, son."

"Two outs, everybody's moving," Cavanaugh called out, just to make sure we understood. I didn't take my eyes off the pitcher. I took my lead carefully, paying close attention to the pitcher's shoulders. They would give him away if he tried to pick me off. I heard the ball make contact with Seth's bat, and took off. When I heard the crowd cheering, I knew it must have been a base hit. Manny almost ran me over crossing the plate.

"Man, you've got some slow get-away sticks, Wails," Manny chided me on the way back to the dugout. "I know white boys are slow, but you're like a turtle."

"Don't you worry about my get away sticks, Manny. You better be worrying about my arm holding up—3 more outs and we've done it," I said.

Miller grounded out and the inning was over, but we had taken the lead, 3-2. It was the last three outs, win or lose, there would be no more.

The first batter rapped his bat on home plate, tucked his shoulder, and looked straight at me. He had as much determination in his eyes as I had in mine. I reverted back to a kid who thought the harder you throw the better. The pitch got away from me and hit the batter on the top of his cleat. He was awarded first base.

Instead of snapping the ball back to me, Posie walked it out to the mound and placed it in my glove. I had made a dumb mistake, and was livid with myself for it.

"Settle down, Corey. Three outs—that's all you need. Keep the ball down and maybe we'll get a double play out of this," Posie said.

As Posie walked back to the plate, I looked out at the crowd. It was the first time all night I had taken notice of the hoards of people that were watching the game. I saw Littleman and all the other scouts; I saw lots of men in university jackets, news reporters, and television crews. This was no small outing. I saw the familiar faces of the other coaches from our conference, and the players that had been our rivals for years. They were all rooting for us now.

At the edge of the fence, closest to our dugout, I saw my father. He was returning my stare. He took his right hand off the fence, and gave me a thumbs-up. I moved my hat up and down on my head, scratching my forehead with the inseam—the nervous habit of mine.

I went the distance with the next hitter, and with a full count he punched the ball over second base, bringing Cavanaugh to the mound for the second time that night. In the name of tradition, but reluctantly, I handed him the game ball. He massaged it in his hands, twisting it, turning it, and pressing on it, while we talked.

"What's the problem, Wails?" he asked.

"I've been struggling with the same things all night, Coach. My curve isn't breaking and they're hitting everything I throw on the inside."

Cavanaugh made a motion back to the dugout, and Duffers got up quickly and headed out to the bull pen to warm up.

"Are you going to keep crying about it, or are you going to do something about it?" Cavanaugh said.

I didn't reply for some time. A minute went by, maybe longer; Posie was standing on home plate holding his catcher's mask in his hand. The stadium was quiet, so quiet, a coin fell onto the metal bleachers and I heard it.

"Let me finish this game, Coach."

I had never asked him that in all my years. There were nights when he pulled me early, and I had wanted to appeal his call, but I never had.

There was silence. Cavanaugh looked back at the bull pen, but Duffers wasn't warming up. He was leaning on the gate with his glove tucked under his arm. It was my game to win or lose.

"Loosen your grip on the curve. You've been squeezing the hell of the ball all night. I can see your white knuckles from the dugout. Throw it like I taught you. And use your legs. That's why you've been running around the field all these years," Cavanaugh said. "Use what you've learned, damnit."

He put the game ball back in my glove, and headed to the dugout.

The tying run was on second base. The winning run was on first. We had no outs, and it was the bottom of the ninth inning. I went through the scenario in my mind. There were a lot of options, a lot of possibilities, a lot of things could happen, almost anything.

I threw the first two pitches on the outside of the plate. They were awfully close pitches for a hitter to watch, but the umpire called them both balls.

"Good eye, Sellars. Good eye," the Charlotte third base coach said.

"Come on you pansy. Swing the bat," O'Conner yelled from the outfield.

I stayed my course, and the hitter stayed his, only the umpire called the next pitch a strike; 1 and 2 was the count. Posie called for a curve. I listened to Cavanaugh; loosened my grip, and let the ball roll out of my hand. It dropped off sharply, just as it reached the plate.

"Stee-rike," the umpire yelled.

Posie shot the ball back to me. "That's the way to throw it, Wails."

Posie got back into position. He opened his knees wide, allowing the third base coach to see his signals. He thrust down two fingers, calling for another curve, but Posie was up to his old tricks, and I knew it. I gripped the ball wide across the seams for a fastball. As I started into my wind up, the third base coach called out:

"The curve's coming again."

I threw a speed ball right down the center of the plate.

"Stee-rike three," the umpire yelled.

Posie stripped off his mask, and shot onto the lip of the grass. "One down, two to go," he called, holding one finger up in the air.

I heard my father from the first base line: "Way to throw the ball, son. Two more now!"

Charlotte was back to the top of their line-up. Their short stop strutted up to the plate and took his stance.

Mike called for another curveball, and I didn't nod him off. I relaxed my grip on the ball, and sent it to the plate. The batter took a full cut, only the ball dropped off sharply, and he swung right over the top of it. "Stee-rike," the umpire yelled.

Mike fired the ball back to me. I wasted no time; the batter hardly had a chance to think before another pitch was coming at him. He swung hard, and barely got a piece of the ball. It came off the bat straight down into the dirt, and dribbled onto the infield. Posie threw off his mask, fielded the ball in a second, and fired it to Stoney at third. It all happened so fast, I myself was unaware of what was happening. The Charlotte coach was yelling his head off at his base runners and the hitter. No one was moving. Hell, I thought it was a foul ball; the way it came out onto the field, I thought for sure it must have hit in the batter's box, or on the plate. With runners on first and second, and the ball in fair play, it was a force out at any base. Stoney stepped on third and the umpire held up his hand, made a closed fist, and called:

"Advancing runner's out."

"First base," Posie yelled. "First base!"

Stoney rifled the ball across the infield to Godfrey, who was covering the bag. The hitter was still standing in the batter's box, wondering what was happening. When Godfrey caught the ball and stepped on the bag, the umpire made another motion with his fist, and called, "Batter's out."

In the last three seconds of the state championship, we had turned the most unlikely double play to clinch the title. It all happened so fast, no one but Posie, Cavanaugh, and the umpires knew what was happening.

"That was a foul ball ump. It hit the plate," the Charlotte coach came out of the dugout yelling. The two Charlotte base runners stayed put on their bases.

It was over—a slow dribbling ball onto the lip of the grass, fielded quickly by Posie, ended the game. The Charlotte coach kept up his hysterics, trying to appeal to the two umpires in the field, but the call was not reversed; the Hillcrest Bulldogs had won the State Championship.

The climax was not at all what I had expected, or had hoped for. I had in my mind a full count, bases loaded, two outs, with a one run lead: a walk would tie the game, a base hit and we would lose, and there it was, a flounder of a play that no one hardly understood until it was over. It was baseball, fair and square, it just wasn't pretty.

When the win was official, the dugout cleared and all the players met on the mound. I took the game ball out of my glove and handed it to Posie. He pushed it away and said, "That one's for you. I've already got mine."

Our celebration ended when the announcer called for

both teams to line up down the base paths. The diamond was lined: blue and white on half, red and gold on the other. Standing on home plate, Cavanaugh received the trophy. It was ours: a small, bronzed statue of a baseball player standing at the pinnacle of a wooden tower. Our dedication to the game of baseball was measured that night; it was measured by a trophy that said we were the best ball team in the State of North Carolina, but no matter how hard I tried I could find no pleasure in it. A dream had come true, only I was not awake to enjoy it.

Chapter 41

WHEN THE CEREMONY ENDED the team headed back to the dugout. As we were walking across the field, I thought about the game, all the games, and all the years I had spent on a baseball diamond. I couldn't help but wonder if I had just played my last one. Deep down, in a place I didn't want to search, I knew the answer to that question.

Cavanaugh was two steps ahead of me walking with Fitz and Manny; Miller, O'Conner, and I were behind them. Everyone was talking about the play; how quickly Posie had made his move.

"Coach?" I called out.

Cavanaugh turned.

"I think everyone here has one of these except for you," I said, holding up the game ball.

"But I'm the only one here that has one of these," Cavanaugh said, showing us his World Series ring. He was smiling ear to ear.

"Was that a smile, Coach?" Manny asked.

The players in front of Cavanaugh turned their heads to get a glimpse of Cavanaugh smiling.

"O'Conner, you owe me 5 bucks. Coach does have some teeth," Manny said.

"A man has to smile every now and again," Cavanaugh said. He reached out and grabbed the ball from me, and clapped Manny on the back of the neck.

"You think I'm smiling because we won this game, don't you?"

"Yes sir," Manny answered.

"You're wrong about that, Manny. I'm smiling because I thought I could make ball players out of you in 4 years and it took me 8 ... Wails, I'm keeping this ball. If you ever want it back, you know where to find me," Cavanaugh said.

When we reached the dugout Cavanaugh told us all to grab a seat. There were smiles all around, elbowing, joking, and all those glorious things that go along with winning.

"I want you men to take a look around you. Look at the faces of the players you've grown up with, the players you've shared everything with, from winning games you didn't deserve to win, to losing games you didn't deserve to lose. I want you to remember the faces on this team, because down the road, you're going to want to, you're going to need to, remember each other. Believe me when I tell you that these are some of the best years of your life—when things can be measured by the number of base hits you got in a game, the number of red boxes you put in a game book, and the number of runs you batted in. These are the glory days gentleman. As much as you may want to, you can't get them back. But there's no damage in holding onto them, they're yours, use them however you see fit."

Cavanaugh opened up his play book. He ran his finger down the page, as his eyes scanned whatever entries he was reading.

"Fitz," he said, and looked up at our star short stop. "Full ride to Wake Forest University ... Manny," Cavanaugh said, looking to Todd, "Full ride North Carolina A&T ... Parker, full ride, University of Maryland, Posie, scholarship, University of North Carolina. Jackson, single A ball in Memphis, O'Conner, full ride, University of Georgia ..." Cavanaugh went through the long list of colleges and professional teams that my teammates would be joining. My name was absent from the list.

"What about Wails, Coach?" Manny asked, craning his neck out, and looking down the line at me.

"Undecided," Cavanaugh said, looking straight at me. I could see it in his eyes that he wasn't judging me, and he wasn't disappointed in me. He understood that something more pressing than baseball was now on my mind.

Chapter 42

FIRST LIGHT LIE HIDDEN IN THE DARKNESS.
The night sky faded. The stars, all except Venus, disappeared into oblivion. Like a carefully rehearsed play, the black backdrop slowly hoisted away and a blue one descended, overlapping as they passed one another. I witnessed a seamless transition.

The funeral was held at sunrise, when life is new. I watched it take shape, as if it happens only once. A current ran through the cemetery, like ripples in a still pond. Nestled deep in the heart of Shenandoah, the cemetery sat on the highest tract of land in the valley. A nimble breeze blew irregularly through the trees, and on the horizon was the moon, resting in a walnut tree. Dodging in and out of the morning shadows, leaves were sailing this way and that, as the land was waking up and stretching out lazily.

"Dearly beloved, we are gathered here today to pay our respects to Linda Ann Wails," the minister began his sermon. His rhetoric was as graceful as the sunrise, and just as quick. He motioned to my mother's sepulcher, and said that she now walks with the Lord. The family and congregation together said the 23rd Psalms aloud, and afterwards, I stood up to read my mother a poem. Emily held my hand as I read:

> So subtle it moves through all that's alive
> So finite it cuts and severs all ties
> It's a force unseen, but I know it is there
> It's the essence of death; it's the burden you bear
>
> You were not afraid, and neither am I
> Your message is clear and will never die
> Within my heart will live forever
> Your greatest lesson, your last endeavor
>
> To live your dreams, to live them well
> For in due time, all our stories will tell
> Of a time and a place, when death will prevail
> A shift in the tide, when oceans will fail
>
> So subtle it moves through all that's alive
>
> The words have been spoken
> The ground is now open
> Sashes of purple and gold will send
> Only your body to its end
> Amen

When I finished the reading the sun was high, a long shadow was cast from the headstone of Linda Wails, and a mourning dove was beckoning a new day. I can recall every detail: the expressions on faces, the wind through the trees, birds chirping and singing in folly, leaves rattling on their branches, the minister clearing his throat, the Shenandoah mountains silhouetted by the low sun, Emily's soft hands on mine, and my father's struggling face.

I remember every detail.

The Time Keeper book club review guide and
an Interview with the author

The Time Keeper Book Club Review Discussion Questions

1.   How do you feel towards Linda Wails in the beginning of the book? How does that emotion change as the book progresses?

2. What are your thoughts toward the relationship between Corey and his mother? Who do you feel is most responsible for the unrelenting relationship and why?

3.   How do you feel about the way Corey reacted to hearing the news about his mother's illness and her wish to make amends? If you were in Corey's shoes how do you think you would react?

4.   What lessons did you take from this book?

5.   Did this book provoke memories of the death of someone you loved? How can you relate to the process of losing someone? In what ways did this book help you relate to that process? In what ways was it different?

6.   Did the baseball games add or detract from the dynamic relationship between Corey and his mother? How?

7.   Who was your favorite character and why?

8.   What is the one thing about this book you best remember – a line of dialogue, a scene, or a thought written in the narrative of the book?

9.   How do you feel about the way death was depicted in this novel? Do you agree or disagree? Why?

10. Which character would you have liked to know more about? Why?

11. While you were reading this book, did you care about the characters? Did you care about some more than others? Explain.

12. Jot down five words that come to mind when you think back on the story.

To order books for your book club, visit: http:\\www.CopperPressPublishers.com. There is a special offer for book clubs on the order page.

An interview with Kevin E. Cropp

This interview was conducted June 20th, 2005 in Wilmington, North Carolina by Hadley Goodman of Copper Press.

HG: I have to ask, why do you use the E. in your name?

KC: (Laughing) I was named after my grandfather, Eugene Collier Cropp. I don't want the name to be forgotten. Besides, it makes my name sound more official. Don't you think?

HG: (Smiling) Okay. Sorry, I just had to ask. What is the most common question you get asked about your book?

KC: Believe it or not, everyone's first question is, "Who is your publisher?" It's a strange question, I think. Since most people only know the names of one or two publishers. But that's the number one question I get asked. The second one is, "Is it a true story?"

HG: Is it?

KC: In a lot of ways, the story is very much true. I took pieces from here and moved them there. I changed some things in the timeline, but the message I attempted to deliver is something I experienced.

HG: What message are you trying to deliver?

KC: That it's never too late. My mother and I waited until right down to the wire to sort out our differences, and to this day she remains the greatest influence in my life. She was a remarkable woman. Had she died in a car wreck or some sudden event, we would have both gone to our graves holding a lot of unsettled emotions between us.

HG: Then why is the book being marketed as a novel, and not a memoir, if so much of it is true?

KC: Some of the book is most definitely a novel, in the truest sense of the word. I imagined a great deal of the book. I took the liberty of having my team accomplish things on the base-ball field that we never did in real life. We were competent, and had a shot at winning the state championship that year. But the fact is, we didn't. We lost in the semi-finals of American Legion.

HG: Did you really play a baseball game the night of your mother's death?

KC: Absolutely. It was one of the greatest games I have ever played. I went nine innings on the mound and was relieved only for the last out of the game; which ironically, was a ground ball hit to me at third base.

HG: So what next? I mean if the book is mostly true, and you are Corey Wails, then what does Corey do next?

KC: You'll have to read the next book. (Smiling.) Actually, the second book is also a novel, but follows my real life very close-ly. Corey goes from North Carolina, on a motorcycle, all the way to Alaska. It's a trip of introspection, as he tries to make some sense of all that has happened. Most of the book is set in the Bering Sea of Alaska, where Corey works as a deckhand.

HG: Why do you think people would want to read about you or your life? What is so unique or special about your experi-ences that you feel they are worthy of a book?

KC: That's an excellent question, and one I have asked my-self a thousand times. I don't think there is anything so special about me or my life that people would want to read about. But my books aren't about me, per se. They are about the message

I am trying to deliver within the pages. The first stage of deciding what book I want to write, is deciding what message I want to deliver. Without a message, there is no book. And that message, or meaning, has to be something universal; something everyone can relate to. In the case of The Time Keeper, the dialogue and emotion exchanged between my mother and I while she was dying is something a lot of people have experienced in their life, or will experience at some point in the future. I just happen to be a writer, and could put it down on paper for other people to learn or gain from it.

HG: Have you always wanted to be a writer?

KC: Always.

HG: What was the first thing you wrote?

KC: *The Time Keeper*. I have never kept any journals or anything like that. I have kept everything in my head for all these years. And I read and read. It wasn't until four years ago that I started putting my own thoughts on paper.

HG: Was it tough? I mean, after knowing you wanted to be a writer for so long, but never writing anything, was it hard when you finally started?

KC: It's very hard work. Any writer will tell you that. But it's just like anything else, if you like what you're doing, it doesn't always seem like work. The good thing is, the more you write, the easier it becomes.

HG: What is your favorite thing about writing? You told me before the interview that you write every day. What do you write about, and do you need some kind of inspiration? Sorry, but I don't know the first thing about the process.

KC: I like to create characters and have those characters do things on their own. It's a hard concept to explain, but when my writing is coming out fluidly, I am hardly the one in charge of the characters. They move by themselves. I simply do the typing. It's like reading a book, but the pages are blank and I fill them in. I don't start with an outline or a rigidly defined plot. I let the characters build the story.

HG: That sounds bizarre. (Smiling)

KC: There's a reason the great writers, like Norman Mailer, have written books about writing named, "The Spooky Art." But I guess everyone has their own style. That is mine—to let the story move without me being in the way. I don't accomplish that all the time, but when I do, writing is a phenomenal experience.

HG: So what are you writing now? More novels, short stories? Have you finished any other books?

KC: I have two other books completed. One of them is about five fraternity brothers spending a summer break from college in Aspen, Colorado. That book is called *istory*. I have almost completed the sequel to The Time Keeper, and I have a third book about a group of hackers who steal stock quotes from the stock exchange and are trading on sure bets. That one is called *Frontrunners*.

HG: I suppose all these books have a message.

KC: Yes. The fraternity brothers on the road is about the X-generation's place in American history. We were a misunderstood generation that are now accomplishing a lot of good things. That is what I have tried to convey in *istory*. It's the most bizarre history book you will ever read. The premise being that every generation has been misunderstood by the generations that came before them.

The message in *Frontrunners* is about the current trends of mingling corporate business with government interests. I think it is a topic worth exploring, given all the scandals that have been uncovered in the past few years.

HG: It sounds like no two books are alike. Are you worried that each book will have a different audience? How will you ever make a niche for yourself?

KC: I consider myself an artist, so I have to create whatever is foremost in my mind. To me that is art. If I go looking for a best seller or a niche market, I will lose the art. I wouldn't do very well like that. I read something a long time ago that I like to remember now and then. It was said by James Michener— "no matter the topic, if you write it well, it will find a market, or it will create one of its own." Something like that.

I can't say if I am a good writer or not, but I do try and I try hard. I spend a lot of time in the review process with my books. I give a lot of books out and take criticism, so by the time you see something I have written, it's been read by a lot of people and has generated some interest.

HG: Is that what you did with *The Time Keeper*?

KC: Absolutely. *The Time Keeper* was read by at least fifty people before the first printing. Some liked it as it was, and some had comments to share. The feedback along the way helped me make it a better book and a better story.

HG: Do you change things in your writing when someone says they don't like something?

KC: Only if I get the same comment from three different people. Then I know I have something that needs work.

HG: I have one last question for you. What is the best thing that has come from *The Time Keeper* so far? What has created the deepest impression or left you feeling good about the book and where it is headed?

KC: So many good things have already happened. I have received letters in the mail from people telling me how much the story meant to them, and how they related to the characters and what they went through. But one event definitely stands out—I was at the beach a few weeks ago when a woman approached me. I recognized her from the book signing I did in Wilmington. She introduced herself and told me that since reading *The Time Keeper*, she has been trying harder to get along with her son. That small comment was worth a thousand words. That is why I write and that is why I wrote *The Time Keeper*. If nothing else comes of my first novel, the years of work have already been worth it. Not just because of that one comment, but because of all of them. With a little luck, *The Time Keeper* might be read by a lot of people who can benefit from its message. I feel like everything ahead of me now is just a bonus.